ONCE BITTEN

SHADOW GUILD THE REBEL BOOK 1

LINSEY HALL

For my friend Caethes.

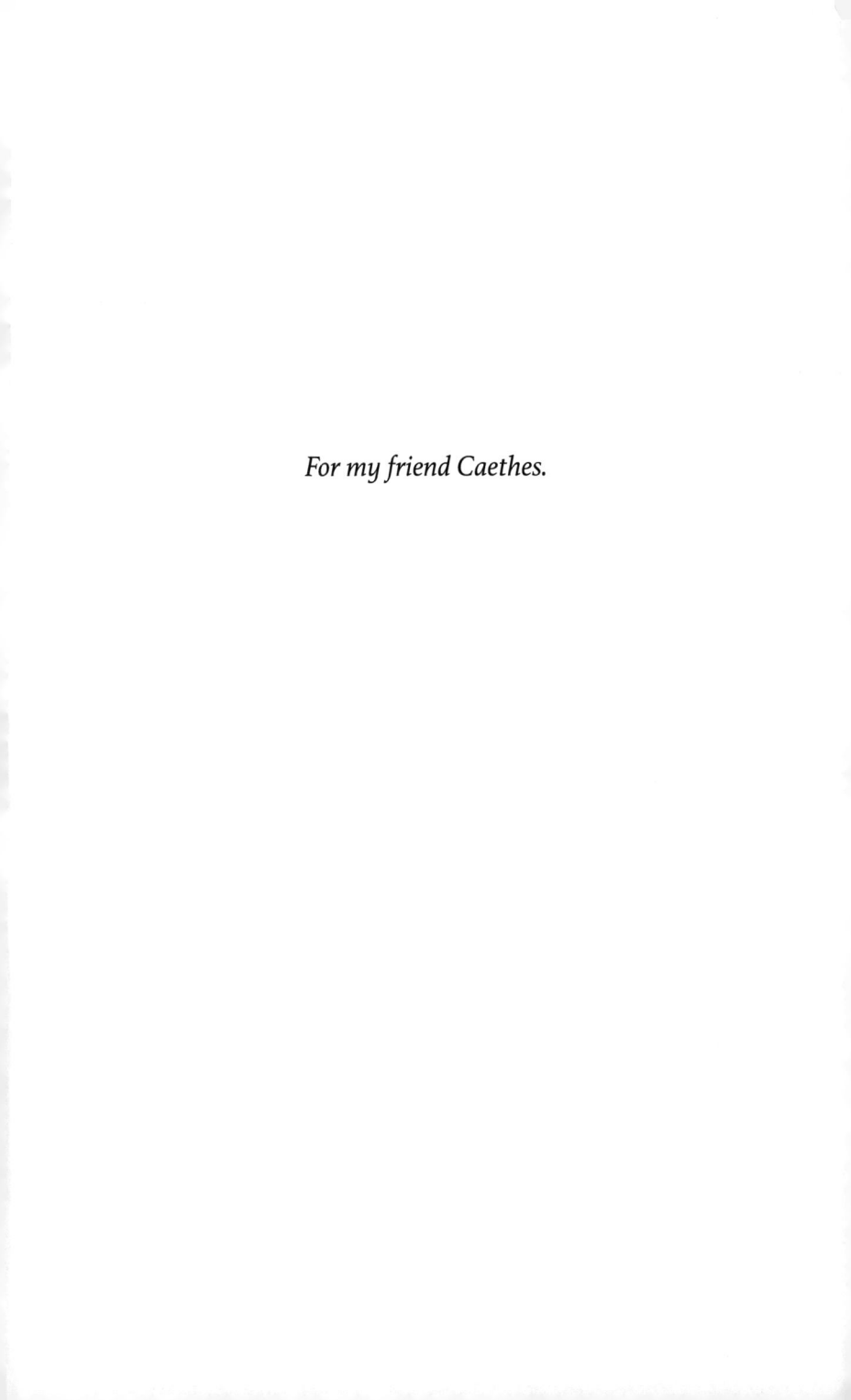

1

CARROW

"I need to get out of this rut." I took a swig from my tiny box of wine—adult juice box, if you asked me—and looked down at my companion from my seat on the fire escape outside my flat.

She didn't look up from her work, busily digging through the rubbish bins squeezed into the alley. I had no idea how a raccoon had made it all the way to London. Technically, they weren't supposed to live in England, but this old girl had made a tidy home in the alley behind my block of flats.

Cordelia, I called her.

Now, when I drank wine alone on my fire escape, it was like I was having a girls' night out. As long as no one looked too hard at the fact that my gal pal walked on all fours and dressed like a furry bandit. Not to mention the fact that she had a real thing for rubbish.

"Cheers." I raised my glass to her, grinning from my perch on the second story of the building.

Who needed human friends when they had a box of wine and a feral raccoon, anyway?

I'd had a real friend once—Beatrix. She was gone though. Murdered last year, and the pain still tore at me. I'd tried to find the killer, but the leads had run cold months ago.

Which left me here, alone with Cordelia.

The night sounds of London echoed in the distance, sirens and shouts since I didn't exactly live in the nicest part of town. I stared down at Cordelia, watching to see what she might pull out of the bin. It was like telly. Almost.

I was too broke to own a telly, so it was good enough.

As if on cue, Cordelia chucked something up at me. She rarely acknowledged my presence. Shocked, I reached out to catch whatever it was that she'd thrown.

My hand closed around an old rag, and a vision slammed into me.

Not again.

I gasped, closing my eyes, as the image flashed in my mind. I had no idea why the visions came, but this one was a doozy.

A man getting his head bashed in.

Murder.

Well, hell, that would get me out of my rut.

The body was still warm when I found it.

He'd been a man once, but now he lay sprawled on the rain-damp cobblestones. His bashed face resembled ground meat.

Pity made my heart clench; nausea made my stomach lurch. I saw death more than your average girl, but I still didn't like it. Who would?

Quickly, I scanned my surroundings, adrenaline making me feel like I might burst. Humans were still animals, and right now, there was a hunter out there.

I didn't want to be its next prey.

Heart pounding in my ears, I searched the shadows of the darkened alley. There were no nooks or crannies to hide in, and the roofs were high above me. Even if someone were standing up there, they were too far away to do any harm. Sure, they might shoot me. But from the look of this poor bastard's face, they preferred another type of weapon.

I turned my attention back to the body. Everything was slick from the recent rain, even him. A tattoo wrapped around his neck, garish and big. A dragon. Blood ran in rivulets down the cobblestones, mingling with the rainwater. I edged away from it, not wanting to disturb anything.

I wasn't a detective—not technically since I'd failed out of the College of Policing—but I did help the local department, and I was still keenly aware of my training.

Except I wasn't going to follow it, because that was how I did my best work.

I couldn't explain my skills, just like I couldn't explain why I'd seen a vision of this man's death and known that I needed to be here. I always hoped to beat the killer to his terrible job—to get there before he did.

I never did.

Death won, every time.

Every freaking time, I'd failed. Even the most important time.

Bitterness twisted my heart. Just once, I wanted to save someone. To help. I'd tried to save Beatrix, but I'd been too late. I'd found her dead in an alley, just like this. She'd been killed the same way. Tears pricked my eyes at the memory of my failure. Sometimes I saw the future, but when it came to death, I only saw the present. Or the past.

I should go. Run. If I were caught standing over the body, it would be the end of me. The cops had found me at the scene of Beatrix's death, too. They would think I was the killer. You could only get caught at the scene of a crime so many times before logic pointed to you, and I was getting up there. Especially when you knew things about the death that they didn't.

But I couldn't go. My feet refused to move.

This poor man had had his face bashed in. I'd been too late to save him, but I could find justice for him. Maybe even stop the killer from getting someone else.

It was that thought that always drove me, no matter the consequences.

I ran my gaze over the man, spotting a tiny burn mark at the base of his throat. It was shaped like a spiral.

I blinked at it, a roaring sound beginning in my ears.

That same burn mark had been found on Beatrix's body.

Holy crap—her killer was back.

Heart racing, I pressed my fingertips to the pale skin of the man's hand. My gift—or curse, depending on my mood—worked when I touched something. I wasn't crazy enough to think it was magic, but I had no idea what it was. I'd never met anyone else like me.

Please work.

I needed to see something useful here.

As soon as I touched the man's rapidly cooling skin, a vision flashed in my mind's eye. I couldn't choose what I saw through physical contact with something—or someone—but in cases like this, I always prayed for a look at the killer.

My breathing heaved as I tried to process the images flickering in my mind.

A tall man with broad shoulders, standing impossibly still in front of the victim. He was cast in shadow, only his icy gray eyes gleaming in the night. A million things seemed to flash in his eyes, and my head began to buzz. I felt like I was staring into the future and the past, unable to decipher any of it but knowing that there was something important there.

I dragged my attention away from his eyes. I was being a freaking weirdo.

The rest of him gave me the impression of stone—like this man had been hewn from granite. Tall and broad shouldered, everything about him screamed strength. He was as powerful and immovable as a mountain, and a shiver of fear raced over me.

But there was something about him that drew me toward him. Something so visceral that it tugged at me. A connection. Heat.

My heart sped up, and my skin warmed.

He was a killer.

Why did I feel this…this *pull* toward him?

Like knowledge. Like connection. Like two stars spinning through space about to collide with each other.

No.

There was every chance he was the killer.

I couldn't see a weapon in his hand—no bat or crowbar or anything for bashing—but he'd been here at the time of the man's death. Otherwise, I wouldn't see him now. He shifted slightly so that light slashed across his face, revealing a sharp cheekbone and strong jaw. His lips were full—the only soft thing about him that I could see. A flash of white teeth gleamed in the darkness, two of them longer than the others. Pointed.

Fangs.

I stumbled back, my hand breaking contact with the body.

Fangs?

That was impossible. I was losing it. People didn't have fangs.

"Come to me." His voice rumbled with low power, and my mind spun.

"What?" I croaked. My visions never spoke to me.

"Come to me." His voice seemed to roll through me, lighting up nerve endings that I hadn't known existed.

Was the murderer really telling me to come to him? *How?*

How was this even possible?

How was any of my talent possible?

"Did you do this?" My voice trembled.

He didn't respond, and his shadowy form disappeared.

I hated to admit what a coward I was, but relief flowed through me. The guy scared the crap out of me. My attraction to him scared the crap out of me.

He could be Beatrix's killer. It was unacceptable

I shook my hand as if to drive off the memory of the

man. But I couldn't. I needed to see. At my feet, there was a dead man with a bashed-in face, and I could help find that killer. Nerves prickled as I touched the body again, reluctantly hoping to see the moment of death.

Nothing. The vision was gone. The man was gone.

"Damn it," I muttered.

My gift or whatever it was didn't come on command, and I'd just lost the thread of the vision. It hadn't been enough to find the killer, though I'd know that man anywhere if I saw him again.

I needed more, and I needed it quick. I'd already called in an anonymous tip to the police, hoping they'd arrive in time to prevent the murder. They hadn't, but as soon as they did arrive, they wouldn't want me rooting through the body for answers. Most didn't believe in my gifts. Hell, I hardly believed in them myself.

Focused, I turned my attention back toward the body. Now that I needed to touch more of him, it was imperative to be careful. I pulled a pair of disposable gloves from my pocket and slipped them on, then began to search the body for clues. I moved quickly, desperate to be done.

My hand had just closed over a matchbook when I heard the shout from behind me: "Freeze!"

Shit.

Cold fear shivered down my spine.

I'd lingered too long.

Please be Corrigan.

He was my only friend with the police, though "friend" was still a stretch.

"Raise your hands!" a man shouted.

My gaze flicked to the matchbook in my hand. The leads on Beatrix's murder had run cold months ago. This was now the only clue I had, and I couldn't read it unless I took my gloves off. I should leave it for the police, but I needed something else to help me find Beatrix's killer.

Quickly, I shoved the matchbook into the inner pocket of my worn leather jacket and raised my hands, knowing how damning the gloves looked. I ran this risk every time I came to a murder scene, but I couldn't stop myself from trying.

"It's just me, guys. Carrow Burton."

One of the policemen cursed, and I knew it had to be Corrigan. He'd told me he didn't want to find me at one of these scenes again, even though I helped him close half his cases.

Slowly, I stood and turned.

Two police officers stood at the end of the alley, their forms silhouetted in the dark night by the streetlights behind them. The taller, broader one was familiar in a good way. Corrigan.

The shorter, skinnier one was just as familiar, and my heart sank.

Banks.

He thought I was full of shit. Worse, he thought I

was probably a killer. He'd made it his life's work to get me for crimes I hadn't committed. At the memories, ice chilled my veins.

A quick scan of the alley and building corners revealed none of the cameras that were so ubiquitous in London. It was one of the most heavily surveilled cities in the world, and this poor bastard had got himself killed in one without government eyes watching.

Just my luck.

It'd been purposeful on the killer's part, I had to imagine. But now there was nothing easy and quick to clear my name.

My arms felt awkward above my head, but I didn't lower them. "It's not what it looks like, guys. I'm here to help, just like all the other times."

"You've never been standing right over a body wearing killer's gloves before," Banks said.

"They're standard issue, just like yours."

"Except no one issued them to you, did they?" Banks was close enough that I could see the triumph in his ratty little eyes. His pale skin was sallow and his expression pinched, but he was more excited than I'd seen him in years.

No one should be that excited while standing next to a person who'd just been viciously murdered.

But Banks was right. I'd failed out of training. I was just a wannabe.

My gaze flicked to Corrigan. His warm, dark skin

looked ashen, and his eyes flickered with worry. "Carrow."

The disappointment in his words sent cold fear through me.

Shit, shit, shit.

"This looks bad, Carrow." His deep baritone, which normally comforted me, was heavy with concern.

"Looks bad?" Banks's voice was high with annoyance and excitement. "Bad? It looks like we caught our killer. Finally."

The satisfaction in his voice made me want to kick him.

My heart pounded. "You know I didn't do this, Corrigan. You *know* it."

His keen eyes assessed the scene. "Then how are you here so soon before us? The body isn't even cold yet, is it?"

How did I explain to him that I was here because I'd touched the wrong thing? A random rag thrown at me by a raccoon, in this case. It'd probably been owned by the victim at one point, though I'd seen no clues on it. One touch with my bare skin, and I'd seen it, along with a location.

I didn't always get a location—a gut-deep knowledge of where on the planet something was happening—but this time, I had.

And I couldn't ignore it. Even though I knew I was already so many strikes down that one more "coincidence" would get me in real trouble, I hadn't been able to ignore the possibility that I could help this poor man. That I could help Beatrix—at least by finding justice for her.

That symbol burned into both bodies meant that a serial killer was back, and I could find them.

I gave Corrigan my most serious expression. "I've helped you catch so many killers, you know I could never do this."

Corrigan's lips twisted with regret.

He'd been a temporary lecturer when I'd gone through training, and we'd kept in touch, even after I'd failed out for insubordination and unusual methodology—my term, not theirs. He believed in my strange talent, or at least, he wasn't willing to look a gift horse in the mouth.

He was the only one, though.

I'd helped him catch killers, but no one else believed me, so they'd assumed I got my info the bad way. The way they could understand. The way that was going to lead to my arrest.

"I'm sorry, Carrow," Corrigan said. "Maybe we can clear this up at the station."

More figures appeared at the end of the alley. Backup. Dozens of people would swarm the scene now, getting to work like busy ants, trying to figure out what had happened and how to stop it from happening again.

And I would be taken to the station.

Then to jail.

Banks's eyes gleamed with excitement. He'd finally won, and he knew it.

As the handcuffs snapped onto my wrists, my head spun.

Holy crap, this was really happening.

Corrigan couldn't meet my eyes, but Banks had no trouble. He leaned in. "I've got you this time."

"You have no idea what you're doing, you idiot."

His jaw clenched, and he looked like he wanted to hit me. He probably did.

My eyes moved around the rest of the scene. I recognized more than half the people—had even gone to training with some of them.

Suspicion flickered in their gazes as they looked at me, and my heart sank. Memories of all the cases I'd helped them solve flashed through my mind. *So many.*

And now I was in handcuffs.

2

The Devil

I tucked myself into the shadows, disappearing into the darkness as I watched the police shackle the woman who'd drawn me into her visions.

Something pulled inside me, hard and fierce.

Protect her.

I rubbed a hand over my chest, confused.

What the hell was this feeling?

I hadn't felt anything like this—much of anything, really—since I'd been turned into a vampire nearly five hundred years ago.

And yet, this human made me want to *protect* her?

Why?

She was beautiful, yes. Pale eyes and skin, though

the colors were so muted that it was impossible to determine shade. All colors were muted for turned vampires. Taste and smell, too. It all came with the curse of immortality, which felt more like being half dead.

But this woman made me feel alive.

She thought I'd committed this murder. I hadn't, of course. I'd killed too many people in my dark past. I wasn't above violence now—far from it. But I didn't crush the skulls of random men in alleys. It was beneath me.

I'd been tracking a stolen dagger—one that I thought had been used on this man. Then she had arrived, then the cops. It was too many people for me. Too many humans.

An insane vision popped into my head—me, storming the scene and taking the woman from them.

It was ridiculous.

For one, it was too dangerous. Not for me, of course. I could have them on the ground in seconds without having to resort to a weapon. But that show of speed and strength would reveal what I was, and the human world must never know what walked among them.

It would be far better if I could get her to come to me. Kidnapping her was hardly a good second impression...especially considering that our first meeting had revolved around a dead body. And I didn't have any interest in unwilling women, no matter how much I might want her.

I settled deeper into the shadows, watching her.

Carrow

I stood in the alley, my wrists shackled and my former colleagues staring at me. I'd completely bungled this. Hadn't been careful enough. Hadn't given myself enough time to search the body.

I should have waited to call the cops, but I'd hoped they'd get there in time to save the victim if I couldn't.

Corrigan shifted, moving to speak closer to my ear. "I'll do everything I can to help you, but…"

"I know. You told me to lie low."

"I warned you, Carrow. I begged you to stay away."

And he had, but he didn't know what it was like to *know* that someone was going to be murdered. I had to try to help them. I couldn't ignore my visions, no matter what it meant for me.

Anyway, I was tough. I'd figure a way out of this.

"Come on," Banks barked. "Fellows will take you to the station."

My gaze skipped over Banks entirely, moving from Corrigan to Fellows, a younger officer that I'd never spoken to before. He watched me with cautious suspicion, as if I really were a murderer.

The body behind me was gruesome enough to make anyone afraid of me.

"Wait," I said. "There's no murder weapon. If I'd killed him, surely I'd have a bat or crowbar on me."

Banks grumbled. "A clever killer like you would find a way around that."

Bastard.

"Come on." Fellows took my arm and led me out of the alley.

As we walked, I looked back over my shoulder at the scene. They were already inspecting the body, trying to find clues to prove I'd done this. They were going to find the burn mark and make the connection with Beatrix's death. I'd also been at the scene of that crime—right after the murderer left and right before they showed up. Talk about bad timing.

And there was no way to show them what I'd seen in my vision: the man standing in front of the victim, tall and broad-shouldered and fanged.

Fanged.

Crazy.

But he'd had no bat, I realized.

Nowhere in my vision had I seen a weapon capable of beating a man's head in. The man with the fangs had been wearing a long coat, though. Perhaps the weapon had been hidden beneath the folds.

The scene raced by in my mind on the drive to the station. Everything was a blur. Processing. Interviews.

With every second that passed, I grew colder and colder.

This was really happening.

My life had been barreling toward this for months, but I'd ignored it. Corrigan had warned me. Show up at the scene of too many murders, and eventually, someone is going to think you're a murderer.

By the time Corrigan left the scene and came to talk to me in the interrogation room, I was frozen solid, a block of ice.

He looked tired as he sat down at the table across from me. There was a cup of takeaway coffee in his hands, and he set it on the table in front of him. His brows were drawn together over dark eyes that gleamed with worry and exhaustion.

I leaned forward, my voice desperate. "I didn't do it."

A heavy sigh escaped him. "The body had a spiral burn mark, Carrow. Just like the mark on your friend Beatrix's body. This man and Beatrix were killed in the same way. We never released that information, which means this is a serial killer. And you were at the scene of both crimes."

"You know I'd never kill Beatrix or anyone else."

"I do."

I slumped back in my chair. "Thank God."

"But it doesn't matter. The team thinks I've lost objectivity when it comes to you, and the evidence against you is substantial."

"What evidence?" My voice was a strangled cry. "I didn't do it, so there should be no evidence."

"You were at both scenes less than a minute after the deaths. So close that you could have been there during them." His voice had turned cold. "A *minute*, Carrow. How did you do that?"

"I see what I see. You know I can't explain it."

He dragged a weary hand over his face. He was a handsome man in his mid-forties, nearly twenty years older than me, but suddenly, he looked like he could be my grandfather. "No court of law will clear you based on your strange visions. That kind of thing just doesn't exist."

A vision of the man with the fangs flashed in my mind. I was certain *he* existed, but I couldn't say it. Not in front of Corrigan.

"I know." I slumped back against the chair, my heart racing like mad.

He leaned toward me, his voice going low. "Banks is going to get you for this. He's been after you for years, and he says he has the evidence he needs."

"What evidence?"

"I don't know, but he's clever and well connected. You're in a bad spot, kid."

"But then the real killer will go free."

"Not as far as he's concerned."

Tears pricked my eyes, hot and sharp. Frantically, I

tried to blink them back. I couldn't show fear. Not here. Not anywhere.

"I can give you one chance, Carrow." Corrigan's voice was pitched so that the recorders in the room wouldn't pick it up. "I owe you for your help with my other cases. I don't want the real killer to go free. And I like you."

"What are you talking about?"

"I don't understand your skills, but I know you can catch whoever did this." His gaze flicked toward the clock set high on the plain white wall. "In three minutes, all the power in the station will be shut off. A fire alarm will sound. And you'll be alone."

My mind raced. Holy shit, he was helping me escape.

"You'll need to be quick," he whispered. "There's a key taped under the coffee cup. Get out of here and find the killer. Clear your name."

"Thank you." Desperate gratitude surged within me. "Thank you."

His jaw was tight as he nodded. "It's the least I can do. But I mean it when I say you need to solve this. Fast. There are cameras all over the city, and every police officer will know what you look like. Solve this murder or go to prison for it."

"You really think that's possible?"

"Banks is convinced he can get you for this, and I think he might be able to swing it. The crimes are connected, and your presence at the scene is the only thing connecting them. He says he has other evidence, too."

"Have you seen it?"

"No, but is this a gamble you want to take? You don't want prison, kid. You've put so many of those bastards behind bars, you won't survive there."

Clear my name.

Or die.

When the alarm sounded, I was ready. The lights cut out, and I made my move. The cameras wouldn't work with all the power out, so no one would see me reach for the key that Corrigan had left under the cup. Whatever I did, I couldn't implicate him. He'd been good to me.

My heart beat frantically as I scrabbled for the key, finding two of them—one small and one large.

The small had to be for the cuffs, and I quickly got them off, then shoved them in my jacket pocket. My heart thundered as I stumbled through the dark, headed for the door. There would be panic in the hall outside—the police station never lost full power. There was a secondary power supply to ensure it. Whatever Corrigan had done, he'd done it big.

A tiny bit of warmth burst inside me. With Beatrix gone, he was the closest thing I had to a friend, and I'd love him forever for this.

I fumbled at the door, my sweaty hands making it difficult work. Self-defense training had proved that I was pretty tough, but I'd never had a lot of experience under pressure.

And this was pressure.

Clear my name or die.

Finally, I got the key to turn and the door to open.

As expected, the hall was chaos. There were no windows in this interior part of the building, and it was nearly pitch black. Flashlight beams sliced through the darkness, illuminating panicked faces. Determined faces.

I turned my head so that my pale hair fell over most of my face and hurried down the hall. I just had to make it out of there before the power went back on.

"Someone call the damned fire brigade!" Banks's irritated voice carried over the din, and my heart started to pound.

If he saw me outside of the interrogation room, all hell would break loose. Quickly, I darted down a side hall, then found the stairs. I was running by the time I reached it, unable to help myself.

The overwhelming desire to flee had gripped me, turning me into the prey I'd felt like earlier that day.

I had one chance, and I couldn't waste it.

I sprinted down the stairs, finally reaching the bottom floor.

All of the exits would be guarded. After all, this was

one of the busiest police stations in London. I couldn't just walk out the door. I needed a window.

Blindly, I stumbled through the dark, hoping to find an empty office. I needed one on the alley wall, since I couldn't just crash out onto the main road. I'd been in this building enough to know which side that would be on. I hurried toward it, heart racing. It didn't take long to find an empty office—everyone seemed to be out of their offices trying to fix the problem—and I shut myself inside the first one I found.

My gaze was riveted to the one large window in the room. It let in the only light in the whole place, and it revealed the tiny alley on the other side. "Oh, thank God," I whispered.

Adrenaline raced through my veins as I picked up an enormous iron paperweight. It was cold and comforting in my hand, and I heaved it through the window. The glass shattered so loudly that I winced, but I didn't hesitate. Quickly, I grabbed a jacket off the chair behind the desk and tossed it over the jagged edges of the bottom of the window.

I scrambled out as fast as I could, getting a couple of nasty cuts in the process. Pain burned through my knee and my hand as I tumbled out of the window and into the damp alley.

The night was still dark, but it had to be well past midnight. I'd been in the station for hours.

Shaking, I raced down the alley, heading for the

back street, which was less busy, though not by much. As I neared the alley exit, I slowed. Sprinting away from a police station was sure to draw too much attention.

My mind spun as I strode out onto the road, trying to act calm as I kept my head down. Cars whizzed by. It was the middle of the night, but London didn't care. It never cared.

Instinct made me head for my flat. I wasn't far, but I debated hailing a cab anyway. Normally, I'd *never* spare the money for a cab. Seeing visions and hunting murderers made it difficult to have normal employment. I was perpetually broke.

But this…

If they caught me…

A black cab approached, the light on top shining bright.

I flung my hand up, and it pulled over to the side of the road. I scrambled in and gave him my address.

"'Aight, lass, I'll have you there in no time." The old cabbie didn't so much as spare me a glance, and I was grateful.

I slumped back in the seat, my heart racing.

I was officially on the run from the law.

From my former colleagues.

Oh, hell.

I shook myself. I had a killer to catch and my name to clear. But first, there were a few things I needed to grab. With any luck, I'd have a short lead and would be in and out before they even realized I was on the run.

Several minutes later, the cab pulled up to my dingy flat.

"You live here?" the driver's voice was skeptical, and I just passed him the coins for the fare without answering.

I climbed out and looked around, senses on high alert. As always, most of the shops had their corrugated iron doors pulled down, graffiti looking like the shittiest modern art. In all the years I'd lived there, I'd never seen half of them open.

But the six stories of flats over the shops were full of people like me: broke, nervous, struggling to get by.

Everything seemed normal, and I raced to the front door, struggling with my key. It *snick*ed open, and I shoved my way inside, then ran up the narrow stairs to the third floor.

I pushed my way into my flat. It was little more than a tiny room with a minimal kitchen on one side and a couch on the other. No table, chairs, or TV. The walls were the color of pigeon shit, and the window had a delightful set of iron bars over it.

Man, my life was lame.

I lived alone, eating ramen and trying to solve murders, but I never managed to save anyone *before* they got offed.

As I glanced around the dismal space, an unexpected wave of grief washed over me. I hadn't particularly loved this place, but now that I might never come back...

I scrubbed away the stinging in my eyes and ran to the tiny bedroom, which was more of a closet, really, with a mattress shoved inside. Beneath the bed, I found the old backpack that I'd kept packed in anticipation of this moment.

My bug-out bag.

I grabbed it and stared down at the ratty nylon.

Corrigan didn't understand my gift, but he believed in it. He knew I wasn't the killer. But he also thought I was an idiot, risking my freedom with every murder I tried to solve.

I might be an idiot, but I wasn't an unprepared idiot. I knew this time might come.

My bug-out bag was packed with my identification, all my spare money—which wasn't a lot—clothes, and the few mementos of my past that I couldn't bear to part with. I still didn't even *know* my past—I had very few memories, in fact. But one day, I'd figure it out. Not today, though.

Today, it was time to run.

3

CARROW

I turned to head back out into the main room, my earlier sentimentality urging me to scavenge whatever I could. Yeah, my place was shitty, and the neighbors weren't fond of me. Or anyone, actually. We were all dead broke and scrabbling to survive in London. But deep in my heart, I knew I'd never be back here. I had a few favorite books from Beatrix that I didn't want to part with, and an old blanket that—

The hair on the back of my neck stood up as the mobile in my pocket buzzed. Only one person texted me.

Corrigan.

I pulled it out and flipped it open, quickly scanning the message.

Carrow Burton, return to the station. The police are looking for you, and things will go easier if you turn yourself in.

Shit. He wasn't really telling me to turn myself in. But he was warning me in a way that wouldn't cast suspicion on him if his texts were ever reviewed.

The cops were coming.

The faintest sound from outside caught my hearing.

They were here.

Screw the books. I'd rather avenge Beatrix.

I whirled around and scrambled over the bed, heading for the small window on the other side. Sweating, I eased it up as quietly as I could and slung my pack over my shoulders. It took a moment to fumble with the iron bars. This was the fire escape, and I could open the bars like a door, but it always made a squeaky noise.

The lock was horribly rusty, and when I pushed open the window, the metal made the familiar soft, terrible screech. It sounded louder than ever before. Every inch of me stiffened. Had the cops heard?

No. Get a move on.

Quickly, I scrambled out of the window. Was that the

murmur of voices out in the hallway, or was I imagining things?

No, they were out there. I could hear them at the door.

Carefully, I closed the window behind me—they had no way to know I was definitely here. No point in leaving them a big blinking arrow indicating which way I'd run. I left the iron bars open because of the betraying squeak, but they weren't visible unless someone stuck their head out the window. Besides, loads of people in the building kept their bars open at the fire escape—it was the best place to smoke.

With a last, brief look back at my old home, I stared down at the alley. I was only one level up, and I could lower the ladder to get down. But that would make more noise.

I should just jump it.

"Just keep swimming, just keep swimming," I whispered to myself.

Then I jumped, landing hard in a crouch. I couldn't head toward the front street—there would definitely be cops out there. But the back street might be okay.

I hurried down the alley on swift, silent feet. The cold night air kept my head clear and my senses alert. As I neared the main road, I slowed and stuck close to the wall.

At the end, I paused and peeked around the corner.

Looked clear.

Even better, a drunken hen party was headed my way. Ten girls, all dressed in sparkly dresses and boas out to celebrate. The bride wore a crown and a sash that said *Last Night A Free Woman.*

"Don't get married then, idiot," I muttered, then cringed. I was being a total Bitter Betty, and these girls were just having fun.

If I were being honest, I was lonely and a bit jealous of their easy friendship. I missed Beatrix.

I joined them as they passed me, trying to blend with the crowd. It was the tail end of the night, closer to dawn than midnight, and they were probably headed home.

Though the hen party was too wasted to notice that I'd joined them, no one else would buy it. I didn't fit in with my black jeans and battered black leather jacket. More like a dour cousin forced to celebrate with them, but it was better than nothing.

I huddled amongst them and let them carry me down the street, glancing back to see a cop car pull around to the back of the building.

They should have covered this exit before going into the front.

Thank God they hadn't.

When the girls turned into a club that was blasting Bon Jovi, I felt my eyebrows rise. Apparently, I'd been wrong. The party girls were still partying, even at this insanely late hour.

I need to get more of a life.

I added it to my to-do list, putting it right after clearing my name of murder. Easy peasy.

I followed them into the packed club, where music blared and colored lights flashed. The whole place smelled of booze and sweat, and the crowd was heaving on the dance floor. My group surged toward the long bar at the back, and I split off, veering toward what I hoped was the rear exit.

Honestly, I'd rather follow the hen party to the bar. I'd have a quick shot of vodka—which I hated, though it definitely got the job done—and then I'd dance the night away and forget my current troubles. Getting lost in the oblivion of this place sounded a hell of a lot better than being on the run from the law.

But that wasn't my life. And I *was* on the run.

"Better pick up the pace," I muttered.

I pushed my way through the press of bodies, aiming for the far corner and a nondescript door.

I was almost there when I got caught between two drunk guys.

"Hey, pretty bird," slurred one of them, his hands going immediately to my hips. He gripped me hard, pulling me toward him.

A streak of anger blasted through me.

"Don't touch me."

I kneed him in the balls, and he bent over with a grunt of pain.

"No fair!" shouted his friend, so drunk that his eyes were nearly crossed.

"Fair? This isn't a freaking game, moron. And no one touches me without my permission."

Especially when I was jumpy and trying to outrun the cops.

I hurried away, slipping into a hallway that led to the toilets. I strode into the women's, ignoring the two girls drunkenly fixing their lipstick in the mirror.

I tossed my pack on the counter and dug through it for my hoodie. Shrugging out of my leather jacket, I pulled the hoodie on, then flipped the hood up. Last, I tugged the jacket on over the hoodie and zipped up my bag.

"You're too pretty to cover your face," one of the girls slurred. Her blonde hair was a wild mess from dancing, but somehow, she'd got her red lipstick on perfectly. That was a handy skill.

"Thanks," I said.

"You on the run?" the dark-haired one asked, her blue eyes keenly assessing me.

I nodded, mind racing. "Bad boyfriend."

Her face fell. "I know how that is." She fumbled in her purse, and I thought she was reaching for more makeup. Instead, she pulled out a small wad of cash and thrust it toward me. "Here."

I stared at it like she was trying to hand me a snake. "What's that for?"

"To help you get away."

The blonde dug into her own bag and shoved a Mars bar at me, then said apologetically, "It's all I've got."

My throat tightened. Drunk girls in bathrooms were the best people on earth.

"Thanks." It was hard to get the words out through my stiff throat. Though my story about the bad boyfriend was fake, I needed the money.

I took it from the brunette, making sure to brush her hand with my own as I did so, hoping that I could see something to help her. An image flashed in my mind—one of a dark-haired guy slipping something into their drinks. Right now.

Bastard.

I gripped her hand. "Don't drink the cocktails you left behind. The tall guy in the leather jacket put something in them."

She gasped. "You know him?"

"I know his type." My gaze moved to the blonde. "You, too. He put something in yours as well."

"You saw it?"

I nodded. Let them assume I'd seen it before I walked in. "Just avoid him."

"We will." The brunette nodded fiercely.

The blonde pressed her Mars bar into my hand, and I took it gratefully. I loved chocolate. Even more, I loved the kind gesture. "Thank you. Truly."

"Good luck," the blonde said.

"Take care of yourself." The brunette threw her arms around me in a hug, and I jerked.

I was the first time I'd been touched like this in *years*. I'd almost forgot what it felt like. I hugged her back. "Be careful. Go home."

She pulled back and looked at her friend. "Let's go. I have wine at my place."

The blonde nodded, and they left the bathroom.

Briefly, I slumped against the counter.

Why did the world suck so badly?

Between the murderer and the bastard with the roofies, this was turning into a dark night.

But the one thing I didn't have was time. No time to worry, no time to break.

I straightened and shoved the money into my pocket, not even bothering to count it. As I strode from the toilet, I unwrapped the Mars bar and took a huge bite.

The guy in the leather jacket was coming out of the bathroom, a smug smile on his face. No doubt the bastard thought he'd find the girls at the table drinking their poison.

He'd be disappointed.

As he neared me, I couldn't resist stepping into his way.

"Hey, baby," he said.

I kneed him in the balls, grinning as he went down with a wheeze.

I was two for two tonight, which was two more times than I'd ever pulled that maneuver in my life. Apparently, it was a night for new beginnings, and I was going to leave a trail of wheezing men in my wake.

He was curled like a pill bug on the floor, whimpering. I swallowed my bite of chocolate and leaned over. "Don't put things in girls' drinks, you tiny-pricked bastard."

I didn't wait to hear what he moaned. There was no time. I stepped over his worthless body and beelined for a back door at the end. It opened easily, and I slipped out into a narrow alley.

Should I risk another cab?

No, too expensive, and I was close to a Tube station, where I could get lost amongst the crowd. I kept my head down so my hood covered my face and moved as fast as I could without sprinting, making it to the stairs that led down to the station. I took them two at a time, debating jumping the turnstile at the bottom.

Nah. Too risky.

Quickly, I scarfed down the rest of the chocolate as I used my Oyster card to get through the barrier, then disappeared onto the platforms. I took the first train that roared up. There was a seat available at the back, and I collapsed onto the worn fabric, trying to catch my breath.

What a freaking day.

The train stopped, and a horde of people climbed

on. It was busy for such an odd hour of the night, but then, it was one of the few lines running. An old woman sat next to me, her white hair wrapped in a blue scarf. Her coat looked like it had last been in style during one of the world wars.

"Bad day, dearie?" she asked.

"You could say that."

She frowned, her pink-painted lips turning down at the corners. "You'd better get that signature under control, or the Council of Guilds will have something to say about it."

I frowned at her. "What?"

She frowned right back, confusion flashing in her eyes. "Ah, nothing. Nothing at all."

She got off at the next stop, and I shoved her words aside. I didn't have time to worry about crazy old ladies. I had a murderer to catch.

And I had one clue tucked away in my pocket.

Now or never.

I reached inside and withdrew the matchbook. It was the first time I'd touched the thing with my bare skin, and a vision flickered in my mind's eye.

The man.

Tall and broad-shouldered, with a lethal elegance that scared the crap out of me. His coat looked almost like a cloak, and his longish dark hair cast his face into shadow. I caught the barest glimpse of sharp cheekbone and full lips.

He still held no weapon, but that didn't mean he wasn't the killer. He was connected to this somehow.

And we were still connected to each other. I could feel it, a tug of recognition. Of desire.

I frowned at the crazy feeling. I hadn't wanted someone in so long, I figured I'd turned to stone.

Apparently, I hadn't. And something about this man made my body sit up and take notice. I vibrated like an engine at the mere sight of him.

"Are you coming?" His voice rolled low through my head.

Holy crap. "Are you talking to me?"

The man in the seat in front of me shot me a wary look, and it broke my concentration.

The vision was gone.

Panting, I put my head between my knees.

That guy could talk to me through my visions. He'd said basically the same thing as last time, but not *exactly* the same thing. Which meant that he wasn't just a shadowy repetition of something.

We were really interacting inside my mind, which had never happened before.

I shivered and sat up. Unfortunately, I couldn't force objects to show me visions. They showed me what they wanted to, and while the visions often had a bearing on what I was interested in, they didn't always. And not all objects had information to share. I still had no idea why, but I no longer worried too much about it.

I flipped the matchbook over and read the back. The letters seemed to shimmer, a fancy ink that was almost holographic.

The Haunted Hound Pub
67 Winslow Lane
Covent Garden, London.

I grinned. My first clue. I looked up at the map plastered above the train windows, realizing I hadn't even checked which line I'd got on.

Not the right one.

I stuffed the matchbook back into my jacket and stood, shuffling between the people to reach the door. It took two station changes and an excruciating delay on the tracks, but I made it to Winslow Lane about two hours later. I ended up having to jump the turnstile on the way out because I hadn't had enough on my Oyster card to get all the way to this stop.

A guard spotted me and shouted. I sprinted toward the exit stairs, getting lost in the crowd, though it was relatively sparse at this hour. I'd been on the Tube long enough that the crowd had changed from the late-night partiers to the early-bird businesspeople. It was easier to blend amongst the sea of black suits, and I ducked my head low as my heartbeat thudded.

The sickly yellow lights of the Tube station gave way to the watery early-morning sunlight. While I'd been on the train, the freaking day had changed.

I could no longer hear the security guard shouting. Thank God he'd given up. My heartrate slowed.

I followed the flow of people onto the street, my senses on constant alert. Anxiously, I tugged the hood around my face. The group that I traveled with poured onto the pavement, and I let them sweep me away from the station entrance.

Covent Garden was beautiful at this time of day, the historic street wide and almost empty near the main market. The businesspeople had all faded off to different parts of the neighborhood, but the Victorian Market stood alone, green metal and glass looking like something from the past.

I turned away from it, slipping into a quiet side street. By now, the cops had got the word out about my escape along with a description.

And if they found me...

4

CARROW

I ducked my head to let the hood fall over my face and stuck close to the brick wall as I walked. Hiding while suspected of murder was hard. Especially in London. Whole place was lousy with cameras.

And for some reason, it was nearly impossible to find Winslow Street. I'd seen it on the maps app on my mobile, but whenever I turned down a street that should lead to it, I couldn't seem to find the damned thing.

Frustration surged within me.

What the hell was happening?

I wasn't bad with maps—the opposite, in fact. I had a damned good sense of direction. And I couldn't find freaking Winslow Street. The sun had risen higher in the sky as I'd wandered around, and my stomach growled.

I didn't have time to eat, but I was starting to get shaky. The Mars bar I'd eaten had been hours ago.

The scent of flaky pastry crust and coffee wafted down the street, and I turned toward it, moving with the determined stride of a bloodhound.

A yellow sign gleamed above a little shop set into the wall.

The Pasty Company of Cornwall.

It was a famous chain, and not the best around, but right now, I was hungry enough to eat a shoe. There was no one in line when I hurried up to the counter and ordered a steak pasty and coffee. It wasn't exactly breakfast food, but it would hold me over the longest, and that's what I needed.

Within minutes, I had my pasty and coffee. I winced at the price, then handed over the money and left. With my head bent low, I found a nook and ate, my mind racing.

As I stood there, a sense of *something* began to tug at me.

I shoved the last bite of pasty in my mouth and frowned around it.

What the hell *was* that feeling?

Winslow Street.

Somehow, I could sense it.

Instinct made me turn right, heading down the road. Another right, and I found myself staring at a street sign.

"It was here all along?" I blurted the words, not caring if it was weird.

No matter how hard I'd tried with my mobile's map, I hadn't been able to find it. But now...here it was.

Confusion flickered as I leaned against the brick wall and kept my face down. The warm coffee in my hand anchored me as I tried to figure things out. Why the hell had I been able to find this place *by feeling* instead of a map?

I came up empty.

Across the street, a broad bank of dingy windows revealed a store that seemed to sell nothing but toilet roll. It was easily the most boring store I'd ever seen. Worse, there was no Haunted Hound pub on the small street that I could see, but I couldn't just leave.

I could *feel* it.

There was a small alley next to the shop, but it was filled with rubbish bins and looked creepy.

Still, it called to me.

What the hell was going on?

A couple appeared on the street—a man and a woman, each dressed casually. They headed toward me, and I leaned against the wall, trying to be inconspicuous.

There was something about the people that snagged my attention. It wasn't their attractiveness, though they were both better looking than average. The woman was pale and slight, while the man was tall and lean, with surprisingly broad shoulders for such a frame, and a dark mop of hair.

They gave me a glance, then looked away, clearly uninterested.

Good.

The woman turned down the alley filled with bins, walking right through them. I barely kept my jaw from dropping, which was good, since the hot guy looked back at me once, confusion crinkling his brow. Then he followed the woman right through the bins.

Oookay.

That was freaking weird.

Heart pounding, I stared after them. The darkness of the alley swallowed them up, and I was alone again.

What the hell had just happened?

Maybe I was going mad. My head was spinning with wild ideas. Had what I'd seen been real?

Nah. People didn't walk *through* bins.

"But they did. I saw it." I pushed myself off the wall and followed them.

I could see crazy visions by touching things, so why couldn't there be weird rubbish bins?

My heart thundered in my ears as I walked toward the alley, my gaze glued to the dark entrance. I should be cautious, but I wasn't. No time for that.

Something strange in the air prickled against my

skin as I hesitated at the bins. I was so close I was almost touching them, and the stench was enough to make my eyes water.

"Here goes nothing." I stepped though the bins, the prickle strengthening, and entered the alley. My head spun with the insanity of it all, but I plowed forward.

The alley itself was dark and gloomy, and reeked of rubbish that wasn't there.

I shook my head to drive off the thought and walked forward.

There was only one door, and it was *not* inviting. The tiny windowpanes at the top were so grimy that I couldn't see through them, and the door itself was coated in enough filth that I could barely tell that it had once been red.

But the sign above the door...

Bingo. *The Haunted Hound.*

I pushed on the door, feeling that same weird prickle against my palm.

What the hell was up with that?

The door gave way, and I stepped into a busy little pub that was about half full of people.

Okay, weird. It wasn't even ten a.m., and yet, all these people were there, eating breakfast on the dark wooden tables. Normally, pubs weren't open at this hour. Or serving breakfast.

Except this place was hidden behind magical rubbish bins, so...

Magic.

Thinking the word made me feel insane, so I drove it out of my mind.

Quickly, I took in my surroundings. It was a nice place, done up in gleaming dark wood and fancy old beer advertisements. The bartender looked at me with curiosity, her green eyes bright. She was tall and slender, with the broad shoulders of a swimmer. Her blond hair was cropped in an overly long pixie that made me wonder if I should hack mine off. It'd be more convenient.

There was something about her, though…a light that shined around her.

Almost like an aura.

I shook my head. Damn it, that was crazy thinking, and I didn't have time for that.

I strode toward the bar, determined to look like I knew what I was doing. I stopped in front of it, and she gave me an easy grin, revealing perfect white teeth.

"What'll it be?" Her voice was light and airy.

What the hell should I order at this hour? Truth was, I'd kill for a cup of tea to settle my nerves. "Tea, please."

She nodded and turned back to the kettle. Most of the bar was dedicated to alcohol—there were at least six beer taps, including some for Real Ale, and shelves full of booze. But there was a pretty silver electric kettle near the sink, and I watched her go to work.

All around me, the air prickled with something I

couldn't identify. It gave me the strangest sense of déjà vu. I swear I'd felt this before.

Breath held, I slid onto a barstool.

I'd reached my final destination—I just needed to figure out why the victim had a matchbook from this place when he died. It was possible the cops could find a link to this location and show up, but as long as the dead guy hadn't had two matchbooks on him, I'd have a little while.

From my stool, I had a view into a mirror over the bar. I could see the patrons behind me, and upon closer inspection, a lot of them looked kind of…weird. I swore that one of them had vaguely green skin. Not in an "I'm going to puke" kind of way, but more of an "I'm from Mars" fashion.

Nah.

But another one looked to have tiny horns peeping up from his hair.

Double nah.

Then I spotted the woman with three eyes.

Well, shit.

I blinked a few times, mind racing. The man in my vision—the killer—he'd seemed to have fangs. I'd thought it was crazy at the time, but…

The woman's third eye, which sat right in the middle of her forehead and was a beautiful lavender color, made contact with mine. She blinked, and it was entirely too realistic.

Quickly, I looked away, my heart pounding.

I spotted a shadowy form near the fire—a dog, curled up on a bed. He was transparent.

Ghost dog.

No way.

The bartender loomed in front of me, and I jumped.

"You all right?" she asked.

"Um, yeah." I smiled, trying to look normal and knowing that I probably came off as insane.

"You're not all right." She said it in the way that a therapist would say it. Or like a really experienced bartender.

"Ah, no."

"Here." She set the teacup down in front of me, then added a tiny carafe of milk and a plate of biscuits.

My gaze fell to them, recognizing the golden rounds. "HobNobs."

"No baking in here, I'm afraid." She raised slender hands. "I'm shit with it. But you'll get Tesco's best."

I grinned. "I don't mind supermarket biscuits."

"Then you're in luck."

I went for the biscuit first, crunching into the treat and chowing down like a professional eater.

"Stressed?" she asked.

I looked up, my mouth full of biscuit, and did my best to speak around it. "How could you tell?"

"You're going at those like a rat in a bin." She raised her hands. "No judgment. You should see me with the

Oreos when I get stressed. I make you look like a novice."

I couldn't help but smile at her friendly voice. It'd been a long time since I'd had friends. Like, forever. My life was gray and lonely and lame, but it was by my choice. I shook the thought away and said, "Right. The stress eating. I do that."

"At least it's not drinking."

"Tea, maybe." I added some milk to the cup and drank, sucking it down despite the heat.

She leaned on the bar, the sinewy muscles in her arms pulling tightly at her thin T-shirt. "Care to share?"

"Ah—" I kept checking out the mirror next to her, and my head spun. I knew how to do an investigation. I'd been trained for it. And that's what I was doing here.

I just needed to get my head in the game.

Except the woman with the three eyes kept meeting my gaze in the mirror.

"What the hell is this place?" I asked.

"The Haunted Hound."

"Yeah, I read that on the door. But, like, what *is* it?"

"A pub?"

"Right. Hidden behind weird bins and filled with people in amazing costumes."

She frowned. "Costumes?"

"Ah…" Subtly, I tried to point my thumb toward the three-eyed woman behind me.

"Clarissa is a triclops demon."

"Demon?" Somehow, I knew her words were true. And while I wanted to put my head between my knees and hyperventilate for about six hours, I didn't have time for that.

The cops could show up here, and I needed to be gone—with my answers—before that happened.

So I did what I'd done when I was a kid and the horror got to be too much.

"Just keep swimming," I muttered. I focused on the task. I had only the vaguest memories of my shitty childhood with my abusive guardian, but one of them was very clear.

I knew how to shove aside all my panic and go tunnel vision on my goal.

Right now, I needed to solve this murder.

Whatever was happening in this bar could wait until I'd cleared my name.

"You're not from around here, are you?" the bartender asked.

"No." I was from London, yes. But that wasn't what she was asking. "I'm investigating a murder."

Her brows shot upward. "A murder?"

"Yeah. Guy with a dragon tattoo circling his neck had his head bashed in." I described the crime scene and nearly mentioned Beatrix, but I held my tongue. Didn't need to spill my guts. "And he had this on him," I said, holding up the matchbook.

Her expression didn't change, but she was suddenly alert. "You with the police?"

Inside, I cringed. This was the part of investigations that I hated. Often, I thought my job would be easier if I could pull out a badge and demand answers. People never understood when you tried to explain that you'd failed out of police training for being a weirdo.

At least, I assumed they wouldn't understand. I wasn't dumb enough to try to explain that to them.

"No, I'm not with the cops."

Her expression seemed to clear, and she looked more comfortable.

Thank God. I could use a break. "Do you know the guy?"

She shrugged. "Not so much. Do you have any other leads?"

"Another man was at the scene. Tall, broad shouldered, silver eyes, with..."

Fangs. Could I even say that?

I glanced behind me at the crowd of weirdos.

Yeah. I could say that.

"He was wearing fangs," I said.

"Wearing them?"

"Yeah. Like here." I made a V with my fingers and pointed to my canines.

"You mean he *had* fangs."

"Sure. Yes." These people were serious about their cosplay, so I wasn't going to offend her by being pedantic. I remembered the feeling that she was telling the truth about the three-eyed demon woman but shoved it aside in favor of retaining my sanity.

"That could be a lot of people. Do you have another description?"

That he was sexy and seemed to be haunting my waking dreams? "No."

"But you saw him?"

"Not well. I don't...remember any more details." And I wasn't going to share that he'd spoken to me.

"But they might be in your head?"

"In my memories, maybe."

"I can help," she said.

"Really? Are you like an amateur hypnotist? Or a police artist?"

"I'm a seer. I can see into your mind. Maybe I'll recognize the guy."

"Um..." Was she crazy?

She crossed her arms and leaned back against the counter behind her. "What's your deal?"

"What do you mean?"

"You seem really on edge. And confused." She gestured around the bar. "By this place."

"I mean...duh? Everyone here is wearing a Hollywood-level costume at ten in the morning."

"There's a cosplay conference nearby."

"Really?" Relief flashed through me. Now it all made sense. I liked it when things made sense.

"No." She laughed. "Of course not." Then she leaned forward, her eyes searching my face. "But I like you. You've got a good vibe. That's why I want to know what's up with you."

"What's up is that I'm looking for a murderer."

"And you've also walked into one of the few shadow world pubs in town and seem to think everyone is cosplaying."

Shit. I was clearly floundering here. "Um…"

"You don't know what the shadow world is." Her eyes widened. "You don't know that magic is real." The last words were said in a hushed tone.

"Should I?"

"You found your way into this bar, so … yes."

"Oh, crap." My hands curled into fists.

"This pub is a shadow world. In between the magical realm and the human one. What's your gift?"

I gave her a blank look.

"Your magical gift. Surely you've got one. I can feel your signature, even though you should be keeping it on the down-low around here."

"Signature?"

"All Magica—that's magic people, by the way—have a signature that's uniquely their own. It corresponds to any of the five senses. Strong Magica have all five signatures. And you…" She hesitated a moment, her gaze flickering as she inhaled. "Have all five."

She looked impressed. Also a little wary.

There was a loud buzzing sound in my head. I didn't want to believe this. It was crazy. But... "When I touch things or people, I sometimes have visions."

"Oh, clairvoyance. Nice. You must be powerful."

"I have no idea."

"Oh, honey, you are. I can feel it." She frowned. "But you've been living your whole life in the human world?"

"Uh...yeah. What other world is there?"

She gestured around us.

"There are bars everywhere," I said.

"It's more than a bar, but I'll ignore that grievous slight to my honor."

A million questions raced through my mind, almost all of them having to do with this place and the world and *me*. So many questions I felt like they could tear my mind apart.

No.

I focused on the *one* thing that needed to be done to keep me alive. It was a terrible thing to learn how to do when you were a kid, but it was the reason I was still here and the reason I was going to solve this damned murder and clear my name.

Then I could learn more about this crazy world. If it even existed. She might be just great at goading people and pulling my leg.

I knew it wasn't true, but pretending it was helped me keep my sanity.

"I'm sorry about the bar comment. And I want to

learn more about this…new world. But I have to solve this murder and clear my name. I have to focus on that first." I felt like I'd break apart if I didn't do that. "Can you help me?"

Something unidentifiable flickered in her eyes, then she nodded. "You're a strange one…"

She was clearly waiting for my name, so I said, "Carrow."

"Mac." She stuck out her hand with a grin. "I like the strange ones."

I grinned back at her, unable to help it. I extended my hand and gripped hers, starting to shake. It was the first time I'd touched her skin, and as usual, I got a read on her. A vision flashed in my mind—the two of us drinking some violently green drink and laughing.

We would be friends.

But then, a strange buzzing fizzled through my head. I blinked, shaking it, and tried to tug my hand away. But Mac didn't let go.

Her eyes widened. "Holy fates, girl. You've seen the Devil himself."

"What?"

"The Devil of Darkvale."

"Who the hell is that?"

"Your killer? The man you saw in your vision? He's the most dangerous—and powerful—man in Guild City. And if I were you, I'd be *very* careful."

5

The Devil

A knock on my office door distracted me from my dinner, an unappetizing cup of blood. I looked up as the door opened and the hostess of my club walked in. Miranda was my second in command, and she knew everything that went on in my empire.

She stopped near the door, a courtesy I appreciated. I didn't like it when people got too close.

Objectively speaking, Miranda was beautiful, with her slim figure and dark hair, but her beauty barely registered on my radar.

No person had registered for me in hundreds of years.

Not until the woman.

"She has entered the Haunted Hound," Miranda said.

"Excellent." My heartbeat quickened.

"Shall I alert you when she enters Guild City?"

"Yes, thank you."

Miranda slipped back out the door, and I returned my attention to the cup of red liquid. I hadn't drunk straight from the source in more than a century. Not because feeding incited blood lust. It was unlikely, given my strength and age. No... I had no desire to touch another person. And it reminded me of the horrors of my past—of all the terrible things I'd done, of what I'd been.

The Impaler.

That was long ago, though.

This was the present, and it brought with it the woman.

What was it about her?

I'd find out soon enough when she came to me.

∿

Carrow

"Just my luck." I frowned at the idea of trying to catch the most dangerous man in Guild City. But... "What the heck is Guild City?"

"I can show you." Mac grinned and looked at the clock behind the bar. "Quinn will be on shift any minute. Then I'll take you."

"Could you give me a few more details about Guild City before Quinn shows up?" I prodded.

A tall figure appeared at the side of the bar, and Mac turned to him, a smile stretching across her face. "Perfect timing."

I turned to look, spotting a man.

He wasn't bad looking, actually. In fact, he was very good looking. Tall and strong, with dark auburn hair and tanned skin. His arms were big enough that he looked like he doubled as a bouncer.

One dark red eyebrow rose on his forehead, and I realized I'd been staring.

Shit.

His green eyes studied my face as he approached. "Got a new friend, Mac?" His voice had a pleasantly deep timbre.

"Yep!" Mac grinned widely and gestured between us. "Carrow, this is Quinn. He's a panther shifter. Big one, too. Quinn, Carrow."

"Hey." Quinn's lips tugged up at the corner in a sexy smile. "You're something special, aren't you?"

What a flirt. I couldn't acknowledge the *special* comment, so I just said, "Hi."

"Afternoon shift is best, you know," he said. "Come

back when I'm on. I'll make you the best drink you've ever had."

Mac slapped him on the arm playfully. "You flirt. Lay off."

He grinned at her, shooting me another look. "Can't help it. Never met a girl I didn't like."

"That's true." Mac rolled her eyes at him, and then looked at me. "Come on, Carrow. We're going to blow this joint and leave this loser to hit on whoever comes in next. With any luck, it will be old Mrs. Wunklebotten."

Quinn laughed, a rich, good-natured sound. "Don't have too much fun without me."

Mac came around the bar and grabbed my arm, pulling me behind her. For the briefest moment, I felt a warm feeling, like being in a fluffy cloud of friendship. Like this was a place and a group of people where I could belong. Where I might not be alone and looked at as the weirdo.

I shook my head, trying to drive the thought off. I wasn't *that* lame. Seriously.

Mac hurried through the bar, headed toward the back corner. Quinn had come from this direction, but it looked like it just led to the toilets.

"Where are we going?"

She looked back at me with a grin. "Guild City, of course."

"Is it in the toilets?"

Mac laughed. "Almost."

She tugged me into a dark hallway. One side was lined with shelves of liquor bottles, but the rest was empty. It was dark and quiet back there.

A frisson of nerves skated across my skin. I trusted her. I did. I could feel it.

But still...a lifetime of wariness left its mark.

In my pocket, my mobile vibrated. Dread unfurled in my stomach as I pulled it out and looked at the screen. A text from Corrigan.

Turn yourself in, Carrow Burton. If the city finds you through a manhunt, the judge will be less lenient.

I swallowed hard, ice chilling my skin. The city was gearing up for a manhunt.

"You okay?" Mac asked.

I jerked my head up, startled. "Yeah, yeah." I shoved the mobile into my pocket. "Just nervous."

"Don't worry, it's cool. You'll see."

She could sense my unease. Because she was a...seer?

Did I even believe this?

"Okay, we're going to see if you can get in on your own," Mac said. "I feel your magic, so it should be possible."

"What do you mean?"

"Press your hands against the wall." She grabbed both my hands and moved them into place. "The ether will pull you in, but you'll be okay."

"What's the ether?"

"It's the stuff that's between everything. Like air, but magic. You can't see it, but you can feel it."

The plaster was cool under my palms, and then there was a fizzing feeling.

My hands sunk into the wall before my eyes. Shock made my stomach drop, but then the air pulled at me. It sucked me into the darkness, and then I was spinning. Spinning and spinning in the middle of nowhere. I wanted to scream, to run.

But I was trapped.

In the flash of a second, I felt my feet hit solid ground, and I stopped spinning.

Holy crap, the ether was strong.

I blinked into the daylight, shocked by my change of location. I stood in front of a massive wooden gate. A huge stone building was built over it, the glass windows winking in the pale sunlight. Two conical towers extended up from the building, flanked by stone walls on either side.

A freaking castle?

I spun to look behind and saw nothing but thick mist.

What the hell?

Mac appeared next to me half a second later, a big

grin on her face. "Looks like you're as magical as I thought."

"What?" I gasped, my mind still doing an insane tornado thing inside my head.

She gestured to the wall in front of me. "You crossed over into Guild City on your own. Only people with magic can do that."

"We're...where?"

"We're in another realm, but we're still on earth. Magic created this place hundreds of years ago within the city of London, a place for supernaturals to live where humans wouldn't find them, and voila!" She gestured to the city wall. "Some say that the Devil of Darkvale himself created it, but I don't know if that's true."

"The suspect?"

She nodded. "One and the same."

I tilted my head back to inspect the enormous gate. This was *not* happening.

But it was.

And I needed to get my head together and not lose it.

Mac grabbed my arm and tugged me toward the gate. "The Haunted Hound is one of the multiple entrance points to Guild City. Once you go through the pub, you arrive at one of two gates that lead into the city itself."

She pulled me to the left, moving away from the

huge gate toward a smaller door that was more suited to a human than a lorry.

"There are guards in the tower," she said, "but they don't check everyone who enters. Your magic alone should be enough to gain you entrance, though the guards will know when it happens."

"They keep track?" My head was spinning.

"Yeah. And if the city is ever attacked, they'll defend. Along with the guilds."

"Attacked? Guilds?"

"Guild City is based on the medieval walled cities in Romania." Her green eyes met mine, excitement flashing within. "Some say that the Devil of Darkvale is Vlad the Impaler himself. That he moved here hundreds of years ago when he could no longer stay in Romania, and he designed a city like the one he left behind."

"So he's...immortal?"

Mac shrugged. "That's what they say. Now touch the door."

Warily, I raised my hand. Part of me screamed to run. But a *way* bigger part of me wanted to shove that door open and race inside. My life on the outside was...nothing.

This, though? This had potential.

I pressed my hand to the door, gasping when the magic sparkled against my palm.

"It's working." Mac clapped her hands.

The door opened, and I grinned back at her.

"Go in." A huge smile stretched across her face.

I pushed open the door to reveal a long, dark corridor. The top was arched, and on the other side, cool gray light shone on old buildings. Wary but excited, I stepped into the tunnel, Mac close behind.

Again, the briefest bit of wariness prickled my skin. I'd spent too much of my life afraid and at the bottom of the heap—first with my "family," and then at police training and in the real world—to not be afraid.

But damn it, I wasn't going to be scared.

Not when there was magic at the other end of this tunnel.

And I trusted Mac. I could feel her goodness. I'd had the vision of us as friends.

I strode down the tunnel, excitement thrumming through me as I stepped out into a small city square. It was surrounded on three sides by Tudor-style buildings, most of them white plaster and dark wood. A few were painted colorful shades that added some cheer through the fog, and brilliant flowers tumbled out of window boxes. Gas streetlamps flickered, giving it an old-fashioned feeling.

"What do you think?" Mac asked.

"It's lovely." Most of the buildings had shops on the bottom, and all sorts of goods cluttered the windows. Here and there, I spotted clear signs of modernity, like motorbikes in the narrow roads and electric lights within the buildings.

In the distance, tall towers loomed at the edges of the city. Each one looked different from the next—some were intimidating stone monstrosities, while others were whimsical wooden structures that seemed to spark with magic.

Mac pointed to them. "Those are the guild towers, the backbone of Guild City. They form the government and provide protection, though that's needed less in modern day."

"Who's in the guilds?"

"Different magical species. There's a Witches' Guild, a Sorcerers' Guild, the Shifters' Guild, and so on. Each of the guilds has a motto and specializes in something. The witches sell potions, seers sell visions. That kind of thing. The most powerful members live in the towers, and the rest of us live in the city."

My brows rose. "Wow."

She nodded. "And everyone belongs to a guild. You have to."

"No misfits?"

"Not in Guild City."

Shit. I'd always been one. Not that I was going to join a guild. I was just visiting.

Mac's eyes widened at something over my shoulder, and she twitched.

I frowned, worry spiking through me. "What is it?"

She grabbed my hand and pulled me with her. "I just saw one of the Devil's men. He's got spies everywhere."

I looked over my shoulder, catching sight of a man lurking in the shadows. He was big and broad, but not in a good way. He had snake eyes. I looked away from him, following Mac.

She led me across the square and down a narrow street. The buildings loomed on either side, most only two stories tall, with the occasional three-story structure tossed in for variety. They all looked like something out of a medieval fantasy movie, but the wares inside the shop windows seemed almost pedestrian until I read the signs. One store seemed to specialize in enchanted clothing, advertising everything from trousers that would make you run faster to dresses that made you float. Another sold boring office supplies but stated that they were weapons. My fingers itched to explore.

"We're here." Mac stopped abruptly and dug into her pocket.

"Where?"

"My place." She shoved the key into the lock of a small green door, then slipped inside.

I followed her up the narrow stairs to the door on the next level. She let us in, then shut it behind her, leaning against it. "We're safe."

"We weren't safe before?"

She shrugged. "Not safe to talk about the Devil. That

guy wouldn't have hurt us. Not in broad daylight without reason. But we can't be gossiping about him in front of his men when you think he might be a murderer."

"Fair enough." I studied her, confused. "Why are you helping me?"

Mac looked at me like I was crazy. "You're hunting a murderer. One, that seems important. Two, it's cool. And three, I like you."

"You don't know me."

"I'm a seer. I *see* you. You're cool."

"Well, that was easy."

She grinned and shrugged. "Being a seer has its downsides, but it's handy for that."

"You can control your gift better than I can."

"Maybe. Our gifts are different, though. It's possible yours is just the way it is—no more control necessary, no more learning required."

"Hmm." I wasn't sure I liked that response—I wanted to have more control—but it didn't matter right now.

I turned to her flat, which was tiny but charming as a hedgehog wearing a flowered hat. From where I stood, I could see the living room, along with a hint of kitchen through a door. The ceiling appeared to be slanted—a product of old age, not design—and the plaster walls were painted a soft white. The dark wood floor was ancient, covered with colorful carpets. It looked like she'd decorated using stuff from a thrift store, but that she had fantastic taste and luck. "Your place is nice."

She grinned. "There's one above that's for rent if you need a place to live."

I thought of my life on the outside—how I was currently the subject of a police manhunt. I had nothing but a cell waiting for me out there, and a flat with some books I'd left behind.

I also had almost no money.

Mac's eyes softened, and I frowned. "Can you read my mind without touching me?"

"No. But you're an open book, and I've been in your spot before."

"Oh." I felt weird but didn't know how to describe it.

"I've got your back."

"Well, thanks?" Making a friend so quickly was weird, but she just *felt* right.

"No problem." She collapsed on the couch. "So, what's your plan?"

I sighed and sank into the armchair. "I need answers, ASAP. So I figure I should go talk to this Devil."

"Even if he's the killer?"

"He doesn't know that I think he's the killer." But... "He can probably see me in the visions where I see him. So going undercover is unlikely to help."

"He's going to be suspicious." She frowned. "Almost no one has the guts to go right to his office."

"I do." Not that I was particularly brave, but I didn't

have great options. "And he wouldn't kill me where people would see him, right? So the office is perfect."

"Sorta perfect. They're loyal to him there, so it will be dangerous. But it's also a bar, so even if he is a murderer, he's highly unlikely to kill you there. Bad for business."

"That's it, then. I take the risk. I need to know why he was at the scene."

"Well, if you insist on going, we can get you some potions to protect yourself. He wouldn't see that coming, and you'd be pretty safe." She looked me up and down. "And we've got to get you ready."

"Ready?"

"When I say the guilds provide protection, I mean that they also protect us from ourselves," Mac said, her voice slightly bitter. "Not that we need it. Sometimes, I think they're too heavy-handed."

"How so?"

"Remember those magical signatures I talked about? How we can smell or hear each other's magic?"

"Yeah..."

"Keep yours on the down-low if you can. Try to control them so others can't sense what you are."

"I'm not doing that already?"

"No, you let them *all* hang out."

I laughed. "So, how do I do control it?"

"You practice, which you don't have time for now. A potion will help conceal your power from the Devil."

"Is he really a vampire? Like, drinks blood and can't walk in the sun?"

"Yeah. A powerful one. He does drink blood, but he can also walk in the sun. The sun thing is a myth made up by humans to comfort themselves." She stood. "And, ah...he can compel people to do his bidding."

"He can *what*?"

"Yeah. He's got some kind of crazy ability to make folks do stuff. It's his voice or something. It's how he's accumulated so much power in Guild City."

I rubbed my forehead. "Of course."

"Just...be careful. It's impossible to fight it, and there's no potion that protects against it. Your only option would be to incapacitate him. Stay alert. If you think he's going to use that power against you, you'll feel it in your mind. You'll have a few seconds to throw a potion bomb and run."

"Oh, man. This is just getting creepier."

"Don't worry. For the most part, he doesn't use the ability. He's a scary bastard, but he's got, like...rules. Honor. He only really goes after those who are as powerful as he is. Or evil."

I nodded, trying to imagine walking into this guy's lair.

Was this a terrible idea?

"Trust me," she said, "there are way worse people in Guild City than him. Assuming he's not your murderer."

"Yeah. Assuming that." I swallowed hard.

"Come on. We'll get you set up with what you need. I'd go with you, but if you get in trouble and don't come back, someone needs to be around to get your ass out."

"Thanks, Mac." I stared at her, unable to process how good it felt to have backup. "Just…thanks."

She shrugged. "No problem. Now come on, we're headed back out."

I stood and followed her to the door, feeling like I was about to walk into an insane world of magic. Sure, it was dangerous. But I loved it.

6

Carrow

"We can hit up one of the shops." Mac led me out of her house and down the stairs. "There's a little local one for things like this."

"Like, a magic shop?" I stepped out onto the street behind her.

"Honey, it's all magic." She waved a hand around at the street.

"You've got a point." I caught sight of a dark shadow across the road. An animal of some kind, small and concealed in the shadows. It almost looked like a raccoon. Like Cordelia.

I shook my head. No way. That was nuts. Had to be a

fat cat. I stared hard at it, and a connection surged between us.

Oh yeah, I was losing it.

The creature disappeared, and I hurried after Mac. She stepped into a store a few doors down from her place, and I followed her into a tiny shop covered in shelves. Thousands of tiny, colorful bottles lined the walls, and a small woman sat on a stool behind the desk. She had brilliant purple hair and green eyes.

And wings.

Holy fates, those were wings. Like real, true wings. They fluttered and glittered behind her back. A gleaming black raven sat on the shelf behind her, watching me with onyx eyes.

"Hey, Eve." Mac gestured to me. "This is Carrow."

I waved. "Hi."

Eve gave me a long look, pursed her lips, then nodded. "Hi, Carrow. What do you need?"

I looked at Mac, a question in my eyes.

She turned to Eve. "We need a suppressor potion for her signature and something from the back room."

Eve's brows rose. "The back room, you say?"

"Yep. And I'm not telling you why."

"You never share the good gossip until way after the fact."

"True." Mac leaned on the counter. "But you love me anyway. Can you help us?"

"Yeah, yeah." Eve hopped down off the stool and went around to a shelf nearby. She pulled a potion down and handed the little pink bottle to me. "That one's for drinking. Come on, this way."

Mac and I followed her to a small pink door just tall enough for her to slip through. She was over a meter and a half, but not by much. I wasn't that much taller, but I had to duck to follow her.

"I'm only letting you in here because you're friends with Mac." She flipped a switch, revealing potions that glowed with an unearthly light. "The witches specialize in a lot of these potions, so they'd kick my ass if they knew I was selling them."

"You do *not* want to get on the bad side of the witches," Mac said.

I imagined being hexed by some old crones and nodded.

"So, what do you need?" Eve asked.

"I'm thinking a freezing potion," Mac said.

Eve raised her brows. "Going somewhere dangerous?"

"Maybe," I said, hoping that Mac wouldn't share my destination.

She didn't.

"Well, this is what you want." Eve pulled a potion off the shelf and handed it to me. "Uncork that thing and dip your finger in it, and you'll be immune. When you need to get the heck out of dodge, throw it to the ground hard enough to break it. The mist it gives off will freeze everyone else in the room."

"Thank you." Dread uncoiled in my stomach. We were at the payment part, and I had no idea how much magic could cost. I had some cash in my bag and the wad in my pocket, but it wasn't a lot. "What do I owe you?"

Eve tilted her head, studying me. She seemed unsure at first, and I wondered if she was trying to read my expression. "What can you do?"

"Like, magically?"

"Yeah."

"I can touch things and people and get a read on their past and future. Sometimes on their present."

"You can't control which you see?"

"No."

"You should work on that. But yeah, if you want, you can trade me in service. Two object readings, one for each potion."

I glanced at Mac for advice. Was this a good deal? She nodded encouragingly.

"Yeah, thanks," I said. "I can do that. Now?"

"No, later."

"Time to take your medicine," Mac said, nodding at the potions in my hand.

I opened the suppressor potion swigged it back. The

sour taste made me shudder, then it felt like all my clothes tightened horribly, holding me in. My gaze flicked up to Mac's. "That's weird."

"Yeah. That's why you're going to want to learn to control your magic on your own. Suppressing potions are no fun. Now do the other one."

I shoved the vial in my pocket and opened the other, dipping my finger into the icy liquid. I shivered and recapped it, then stored it in my pocket.

An idea flared. "What about a truth potion?"

"Oh, those are hard to come by." Eve chewed her lip. "I don't have any on hand, but I can make one and give it to you later. It won't be powerful, and I only have enough ingredients for one. Still, that should get you a single answer from a person . . . if they're willing."

"And if they're unwilling?"

"You're shit out of luck. Like I said, truth potions are super rare and hard to come by. That's why I don't keep them in stock."

"Okay," I said. "I'll take it. Who knows? It might come in handy in the future."

"No problem. I'll let you know when it's done."

"Thank you."

"Ready to visit the Devil's lair?" Mac asked. "I can take you to the entrance."

"His lair?"

"It fits, doesn't it?"

"Yeah."

We said our goodbyes to Eve and headed for the door. A shiver ran down my spine. I looked back and found the raven watching me.

"What's with the bird?" I asked Mac.

"I'm not sure. Eve says she doesn't see it, but I don't buy it." She shrugged. "I want to push her for more info, but I don't."

"Clever."

"You sure you don't want to move in over my place?" she asked.

"Um…"

"I can tell you're on the run from something, and this is a good place to lie low. And it's fun here." She led me down the narrow streets.

"How can you tell I'm on the run?"

"Like knows like."

I nodded. It would be good to have friends. And damn if this place wasn't cooler than normal London. "I don't know if I could afford it."

"You can." She squeezed my shoulder. "You've got a powerful gift. You could definitely set up shop with it."

"There seem to be a lot of magical shops, though."

"Not a lot with skills like yours, if you're hunting a murderer. You could be a PI." She made finger guns with her hands, and somehow, it was charming. "Magic PI, here to solve the case. Or a bounty hunter."

I laughed. "Let me catch this murderer first."

"Well, you're about to have your chance."

We walked down the charming streets, passing supernaturals of all sorts. My head spun from the variety.

"What was Eve?" I asked. "She had wings."

"She's Fae. Without a court, of course. Since she lives here."

"What does that mean?"

"All Fae are members of Courts. Magical—magical realms located all over the earth. There are Sea Fae, Fire Fae, Unseelie and Seelie Fae. Lots of others, too. If they leave their Courts, they can go a bit insane if left on their own."

"Insane?"

"Yeah. They need the company of other Fae. At least a little. So a lot of them come here and join the Fae Guild."

"Eve lives in her guild tower?"

"No. She's like me—a loner. It's enough for her to be a member of the guild. She lives next to me, actually."

"That's cool."

Mac stopped, and I realized we'd appeared in another grassy square at the edge of town. We stood amongst the shops and restaurants on one side, staring at the tower on the other. It was situated in the middle of the huge wall that surrounded Guild City, and it was easily one of the creepiest towers I'd seen, black-painted stone with windows of red glass that glinted in the sunlight. The one door was guarded by two huge men who looked like bouncers.

"Which guild is this?" I asked.

"This is the only tower in town that doesn't belong to a guild. It belongs to the Devil."

"My vampire suspect? How'd he get a guild tower to himself?"

"No one is sure. But he's had it forever, and no one dares take it from him."

"If he's some kind of criminal kingpin, then why doesn't the local government do anything about it?"

"Do what? He's more powerful than they are." She shrugged. "And no one can prove anything. Most believe he just owns a few clubs around town."

"Does he do really bad stuff? Like human trafficking and murder?"

"Until now, with this murder thing, I haven't heard of him dealing in anything super evil. Which is why I'm letting you go in there alone. But he's done bad stuff—mostly dealing in magic, which is carefully regulated by the Council of Guilds. They keep much tighter control on things in here, compared to magical cities in the rest of the world."

I nodded. "Okay, I can handle a mostly bad vampire kingpin, no problem." I laughed, low and surprised. "My life has turned insane."

"It's always been insane. You just haven't seen it."

"Good point." It's not like my ability to read objects was new. "Thanks, Mac."

"Sure thing. If you're not out in an hour, I'm coming in."

"Don't risk yourself."

"I do what I want." She gave the last word a lilt that made me smile.

I turned and strode across the grass, committed to my plan. He'd seen me at the murder scene—it had been clear in my visions—so trying to trick him wasn't going to work. I could still be crafty, but I'd be upfront.

And I had these two handy potions, one in me and the other in my pocket.

The two bouncers glared as I approached. Their dark suits were pressed and made of a tough, tactical material. It was a pretty cool look, actually. Not that I got out much to determine what was cool. My only girls' night out had been a few hours ago when I'd sneaked into the club with the hen party.

Both men were eerily handsome, with powerful builds and an almost animal grace.

"Reason for entry?" the guy on the right asked.

Inspiration struck. "Your boss wants to see me."

It was true, after all. He'd called me to him.

He raised his wrist and spoke into the charm there, his words low and muffled. After a moment's pause, he turned, opening the door. "He's waiting for you."

Maybe I was imagining the ominous tone to his voice, but I thought not.

The interior of the building was cool, dark, and quiet. The stone floor gleamed with a dark light, like onyx set with stars. The walls themselves were papered in dark velvet, and the lights were sharp and modern.

A slender woman with milk-pale skin and straight dark hair waited for me. Her black dress molded to her form, looking more appropriate for evening than midafternoon.

"Come." Her voice was smooth and even. "I'm here to take you down."

She didn't call my quarry the Devil, and I wondered if his staff called him that or just people like Mac. My heart thundered in my ears as she led me through the only door in the room, which opened into a beautiful nightclub.

The whole place reeked of money and power, with magnificent furnishings and chandeliers that glittered with golden light. The tables were carved of black stone, and the enormous stage was silent. Though there were a few people in the place, they appeared to be speaking quietly.

Having meetings? Magical mob meetings?

Holy crap, what had I gotten myself into?

Fortunately, none of them looked at me, and I kept my head down as I followed the woman. Despite my posture, I made a point to take in all the exits—three—and everyone in the room. If I had to run for it, I wanted to know exactly where I was going and get out fast.

The woman led me through one of the exits, entering a hallway that was simply decorated with dark gray paint and plain light fixtures. As we walked, I grew oddly disoriented.

She turned around and caught my eye. "Don't worry about how you're feeling. It's a spell to make it hard to find your way back in, but it should do no lasting damage."

"Of course." I tried to act like that was normal, but it sure as hell wasn't.

By the time we reached a large door at the end of a hallway, I was completely lost. Even if I did try that freezing potion, I might end up stuck in this hallway forever.

The woman knocked quietly, then waited. I heard nothing, but she nodded to herself and pushed open the door.

Memories of the man in my vision streaked through my head, and my heart began to pound even faster.

I was going to see him.

Holy crap, I was about to walk into the den of a possible murderer. Who could do mind control.

But I had the freezing potion. And I could handle myself.

More importantly, I needed answers if I wanted my life back. And I wanted to see this guy.

I sucked in a deep breath and followed her in.

The first thing that struck me was his stillness. He sprawled elegantly in a chair behind a wide desk, his form so motionless that he could have been carved of ice.

The second thing was his size. His power. Despite the fact that he was sitting, it was clear that he was tall and leanly muscled. He had the tightly leashed power of a large jungle cat, reclined and relaxed...until he pounced. When he did, you'd be dead.

I carefully kept my gaze averted from his, hoping to prevent him from controlling my mind. Still, I managed to get a good look.

His face was cast in shadows, but the parts that I could see were almost too beautiful to be real. He was a predator who lured you with his looks. Slightly long dark hair that gleamed in the light. Strong, sharp jaw, full lips, high cheekbones, and glinting silver eyes. Everything about him was cold, but in a way that heated me up inside.

That connection I'd felt earlier flared to life, tugging me closer. Everything within me sat up and took notice. I wanted to spend hours staring at him, despite the fact that he scared the crap out of me.

No.

Idiot. He might be a murderer. He might be *Beatrix's* murderer.

I had a hard time believing it, though. Wouldn't I feel something if I were looking her murderer in the eye?

Yes. I would.

Still, I was terrified of him. He was a vampire, for God's sake. Killing was in their DNA, according to the movies I'd seen. I couldn't count on my gut feeling that I would recognize Beatrix's murderer when I saw him. That kind of crazy, could get me killed.

I was so not here to get murdered myself, no matter how powerful the magical connection between us.

Because that's what this had to be—magic.

I'd never lost my mind over a man like this before.

Behind him, someone shifted. Two guards—both huge, hulking men standing against the wall. They had the same leonine look as the guards out front, like they had the souls of animals—lions or panthers or something. I hadn't noticed them before, but I couldn't blame myself. The real threat here was the Devil of Darkvale. He was seated and impeccably dressed, but I'd seen enough deadly people in my life to know he was dangerous.

The guards could do the dirty work, sure. But it was the Devil you had to watch out for. He was all tightly leashed power, but when he released it…

He studied me in silence, then raised his hand. The

guards melted into the shadows at the edge of the room, disappearing.

"You've come to me," the Devil said, his voice dark and low.

There was a quiet arrogance there—the kind that kings carried. Kings who had gained their power with sweat and blood and charm and knew that they would never suffer defeat because the world was theirs to control.

I swallowed hard, trying to force back that strange combination of attraction and fear.

Please don't use your mind control. "What do you know about the murder of the man with the dragon tattoo on his neck?"

He tilted his head, the shadows slashing across his face and making him look even more dangerous. He gestured to the chair in front of his desk. "Please, have a seat."

And lose the ability to chuck my potion and run? Hell, no. "I'm fine, thanks."

He rose from his chair, graceful and dangerous, and moved around to the front of his desk. Every bit of me screamed to move, but I held my ground. His gaze flicked to my neck as if he could see my violent heartbeat.

Vampire.

I kept my gaze averted.

Instead of approaching, he leaned against his desk,

facing me. There was a good two meters between us, but it felt like a handbreadth. I could detect the barest hint of his magic—the scent of a fire and the sound of thunder—but it was well under control.

Everything about him was well under control but, somehow, I knew...beneath the surface, there was more than ice.

"Did you kill the man in the alley?" I asked, wishing I already had that truth serum.

"No."

"That's it? Just...*no*?"

"Just no." He strode toward me, his movement impossibly smooth.

My heartbeat thundered as he approached, and my skin chilled. It took everything I had to hold my ground, but I refused to run. There was too much on the line here, and he was an apex predator. I couldn't show fear, or he would attack.

Even if that wasn't true, I couldn't bear to let him know I was afraid.

Instead of coming straight for me, he moved past, so close that I could smell the fire of his scent. Every bit of me tightened as I turned to follow his back with my gaze, and my shoulders relaxed when he went to the sideboard on the other side of the room.

He looked back at me over his shoulder. "Coffee?"

"Um...no." I wasn't going to drink a possible murderer's coffee.

He poured himself a cup, and the wild thought burst into my head that he also drank blood.

But where were his fangs?

My gaze flicked to his mouth, but I saw none. When I looked at his eyes, I realized that he was smiling at me. Not a big smile, but he was definitely amused.

7

The Devil

I watched the woman. She stood still as a hare spotted by a fox, her gaze carefully averted from mine. My body screamed with an awareness I hadn't felt in years. Hell, that I had never felt.

What was it about her that made me feel alive? She had eyes that seemed to see right through me, though she wouldn't make eye contact. The back of my neck prickled as if I were being watched from all angles. Like she could see right to the heart of me and all the terrible things I'd done.

Was that what so intrigued me?

No.

There was a connection, one that I'd never felt before.

And I wanted to sink my fangs into her pale neck and feel every bit of it.

I wanted to touch her. It was something I hadn't felt in hundreds of years, and she ignited it.

I reached out for her mind, attempting to make contact in a way that would compel her to do my bidding. I wouldn't use it in an unscrupulous way—I never did that with women—but I wanted to feel that connection. I wanted to make her look at me.

She didn't comply.

How was that possible?

Did my power not work on her?

She stiffened her spine and demanded, "What do you know about the man in the alley?"

"You could see me there, then?"

She nodded. "I saw you."

"But you weren't there. Not when I was." I studied her, trying to get a hint of her magical signature. It was locked down tight, though not by her own effort. I detected the faintest hint of a suppressor potion.

She wasn't used to keeping her signature locked down, which confirmed that she wasn't from Guild City. Everyone here knew how to keep their magic under tight lock and key—the Council of Guilds demanded it. Their strict control of magic in the city was half of what made it possible for me to run my business. Smuggling boomed under strict law and governments. It was perfect for my particular talents.

But then, I'd already known she wasn't from my city. I knew everything that went on in this part of London. It was impossible not to be painfully aware of her.

"Well?" I prodded. "You weren't in that alley at the same time I was. I'd have noticed you. But you made a connection with me there."

She nodded sharply, and I spotted the indecision in her eyes. Finally, she said, "I saw you in one of my visions."

"Does that happen normally?" If my power didn't work on her, then she was special to me. I wanted to know if I was special to her.

"Tell me about the body in the alley."

I grinned, liking that she evaded my question. She wasn't an easy woman, and I found that it appealed to me. "If you were worried that I was the murderer, why come here?"

"Because I can take care of myself."

I believed it—for the most part. She could handle herself around others, yes. Still, I could have her underneath me in seconds if I wanted.

But no, that monster was dead inside me now. Killed by my own hand.

These days, I found I preferred the chase.

And no matter how much the citizens of Guild City believed otherwise, I wasn't a monster. Not all of me.

"No." I tilted my head to better study her. "You came because you are backed into a corner."

She scowled at me but didn't press for more answers. "Tell me about the man in the alley."

"Persistent, aren't you?"

"You have no idea."

"I'm not the murderer." I sipped the coffee and watched her from my spot across the room.

"I'm not sure I believe you."

"You're not dead yet, are you?"

She scoffed. "Just because you killed him doesn't mean you'll kill me. Not right away, at least. You might want me for something."

Want me for something.

An unfamiliar heat blossomed inside me. Yes. I very much did. But not for killing.

I shoved the thought to the back of my mind. Now wasn't the time for that.

"Why are you tracking the murderer?" I asked.

Her lips tightened, and I could see the thoughts behind her eyes. She was debating how much to tell me. Clever. I trafficked in information as much as anything, and the wise ones knew it was dangerous to tell me things.

Except...

I couldn't hurt her.

At the mere thought of it, the strangest sensation of protectiveness roared inside of me, a beast bigger than my need to feed. Bigger than anything.

"Why?" I demanded, suddenly more interested than I had been.

"The police think I killed him, and I need to clear my name." Surprise flashed over her face, almost as if she couldn't believe she'd told me that.

"You live in the human world?"

"I do."

"But…why?" Why would *any* supernatural ever do that? I couldn't imagine hiding what I was.

"We're not here to talk about me."

"Oh, but I'd like to." And I meant it. I wanted to know everything about her, even as I marveled at this new interest. I hadn't been interested in much of anything in years.

But her…

She ignited it.

I tried again to compel her to look at me, but she didn't.

I still couldn't control her.

She watched the space just to the left of me, her muscles tense and her expression wary. "You've been dancing around this. Just give me some answers."

She was right. The frustration seemed to bubble inside her, and I didn't want to drive her off.

Anyway, I was interested in the murder, too.

"I don't know who killed the man. I was there just after it happened." Her arrival on the scene had driven me off, in fact. I'd left before I'd seen her coming, once I'd sensed someone else was arriving on the scene. If I'd seen her, I would have stuck around longer. Instead, her vision had snared me once I was several streets over, dragging me back to the scene of the crime—or at least dragging my consciousness back. Such interest in another was uncharacteristic of me.

"There's really nothing you can tell me?" She crossed her arms over her chest. "Because I find that very hard to believe."

"Check his organs. See if anything is missing." I hadn't had time to do it myself.

Confusion twisted her features, and her eyes darkened with fear. "What? Missing? There was no blood or wound."

"There doesn't need to be."

"You're not talking about some long-ago surgery, are you?"

"No. He'd be missing an organ that he needs. If he's missing one at all." I shrugged. "It's a hunch, but it could be inaccurate."

"So the smashed head wasn't the death wound?" She shifted back from me slightly, igniting my instinct to pursue. The desire to stalk her surged to life, and I forced it back, hating it just a little.

"How do you know so much about this if you're not the murderer?" she asked.

"A weapon was stolen from me, and I was tracking it. I believe it was used on the victim, but not by my own hand."

"And if it was, then one of his organs might be missing?" Her breathing quickened, as if discussing the murder—with the possible murderer, as far as she was concerned—was scaring her.

Her fear made my heart thud faster, and I stepped toward her, unable to stop. A vision of pressing her against the desk, of feeling her softness against me, flashed into my mind. In my head, I could hear her cry out, feel the warmth of her skin under my lips, her flesh under my fangs.

Desire pulsed inside me, heating my skin and quickening my heart. I hated the instinct that surged to arousal—to catch, to subdue, to take. It was nearly as old as I was, but I hadn't always hated it. Once, I'd reveled in what I'd been made into.

No longer. Yet she ignited it in me, and I had no idea what to do about that.

Carrow

. . .

The Devil of Darkvale stepped toward me, his dark eyes flashing with something that made me shiver. Fangs had appeared in his mouth, and his eyes glinted with an icy heat that mimicked the hot and cold streaking through me.

I jerked my gaze from his, my mind prickling with awareness. Fear tightened everything inside me, but...

I liked it, too.

And that scared me as much as anything. It was insane.

He stepped forward, so slow and sure. He'd become a cobra, and me the mouse.

Nope!

I shoved my hand into my pocket and withdrew the potion bomb. My movements were faster than my brain, and before I'd realized it, I'd chucked the bomb at his feet. The cloud of pale blue dust poofed up, enveloping him.

I ran, not even waiting to see if it had worked. Heart pounding, I sprinted for the door. It opened easily, and gratitude welled within me when I realized there were no guards.

Unable to help myself, I shot one last look into the room behind me. The Devil was frozen mid-step, looking perfect and terrifying at the same time. It made my heart thunder all the harder, and I spun.

I'm getting the hell out of here.

I ran down the hall, pursued by the demon of fear.

Visions of him catching me flashed in my mind. Once, I heard people coming from an adjacent hallway, and I slowed.

I couldn't be caught. Right now, the only thing I had on my side was stealth. No one knew that I'd frozen the Devil. With any luck, I'd get out of there before they realized it.

The bright sun outside was a siren call, and I followed it. The halls were as confusing as they had been when I'd come in. Whatever spell they'd used to mess up my mind had worked. But I kept striding confidently down the hall as I searched for the way out.

At one point, I passed two women in tight pencil skirts and black shirts. Both looked hot as hell and sharp as knives, their red lips matching their upswept hairdos that mimicked styles of the past. As they passed, they looked at me, heads tilted in confusion. I gave them a tight nod, pretending that I knew what I was doing. Somehow, I managed to keep my heart from smashing out of my chest and smacking them in the face.

They passed by, and I moved faster.

Finally, I found the nightclub part of the tower. It was early in the day and still fairly empty, and no one paid attention to me as I strode through. In the small entry chamber between the bar and the outside, the hostess stood at her podium. I stepped into the room, and she blinked at me, clearly confused.

"Thanks, it was great." I nodded at her and strode quickly to the door.

"But the Devil—"

I didn't hear the rest of her words because I was sprinting outside. The two guards looked at me, their sharp eyes seeing too keenly.

Did they know I was on the run?

The one on the left raised his wrist to his lips, and I remembered him speaking into a device there.

He was calling the Devil.

The other reached for my arm, and I flinched away.

He was too fast. His hand closed around my bicep.

"Hey!" I tried to jerk away, but he was too strong.

Movement flashed in front of me, everything happening so quickly that I almost couldn't process it. A woman with short blonde hair appeared, and then came a flash of light and faint blue dust. It enveloped me, nearly blinding me. The guards froze solid, totally unmoving.

"Come on!" Mac's voice sounded through the dust.

I blinked, trying to pull away from the guard. His grip was like iron, and it was nearly impossible to break.

Mac appeared through the mist. "You're killing me. Come on."

I gripped the frozen guard's hand tight and yanked at the fingers, finally breaking free.

"This way." Mac turned and disappeared through the blue mist.

I followed her, coughing as we ran out into the open square. The mist dissipated, and I sucked in a deep breath. "Thanks, Mac."

"No problem." She grinned at me.

"Was that the same freezing potion I used?"

"Yeah. Eve had an identical one, and since you'd already made yourself immune..."

"It worked." I rubbed my forehead, heart still pounding as we exited the square and entered a narrow street. "Seriously. You saved my bacon. Thank you."

"Anytime." She looked over her shoulder, expression wary. "No one is coming yet."

I looked back, still able to see the Devil's tower across the square. It looked silent and empty, the two guards out front standing eerily still. "When will they wake up?"

"Three or four hours, maybe," Mac said. "Give or take."

"Same for the Devil?"

"Maybe less for him. Eve said that stronger supernaturals can break free more quickly."

"Shit."

"Do you need to get out of town?"

"I don't know." Memories flashed in my mind. "I think he wanted to...bite me."

"*Bite* you?"

"He's a vampire, right? Don't sound so surprised."

"Yeah, but I've never heard of him biting anyone.

He's pretty famous around town for not sampling the wares at his club. Or any of the blood bars, for that matter."

I cringed. "Blood bars?"

"Not as creepy as you'd imagine. Mostly."

"Do vampires, um…drink you to death?"

"They can. Definitely. But they don't always."

"So they aren't compelled to?"

"When they're recently turned, they might be. But not older ones."

"Not the Devil, then."

"No. But I'd still be wary of him."

"Hell, yeah."

She stopped in front of her green door. The savory scent of roasted meat wafted toward me, and I realized that Mac's flat was right over a kebab place. How had I not noticed that?

"He didn't try to control your mind?" she asked.

"I don't think so. I thought my head might have felt a bit weird, but I didn't feel like I was doing anything I didn't want to do."

"Hmm. You'd have felt it."

"Maybe it doesn't work on me."

"Then that would make you very special, indeed."

Special to the Devil? I wasn't sure I liked my odds of coming out of that alive.

"Come on up," Mac said. "We need to get off the street."

"He could get us out here?"

"If he really wanted to."

"Lead the way." Next time I saw him—*if* there was a next time—I needed to be in complete control.

Honestly, I hoped he wasn't the killer so I wouldn't have to see him again.

Mac unlocked the door and hurried up to her flat. I followed, stepping into the welcoming interior behind her. It was as small and cluttered as we'd left it, but after my brush with death at the Devil's place, it looked extra good to me.

Mac spun around. "Okay. It's basically dinnertime, and I'm starving. We need food for this." She went to the small window that looked out over the street and pushed it up. A cool breeze rushed in, and she glanced over her shoulder at me. "What do you like for a kebab takeaway?"

"Anything, really."

"Doner kebab, then?"

My stomach grumbled at the mention of the roasted meat. "That'll do."

"Coming right up." She grabbed a little notepad off the table next to the window and scrawled some words onto it. Then she tore it off and picked up a bucket that sat beneath the window. A rope had been tied around the bucket's handle. She tossed the paper in the bucket, then lowered it out the window. After a few seconds, she wrapped the other end of the rope around a metal gizmo that was attached to the wall. A cleat, I thought it was called, a fixture normally found on docks.

She turned back to me, a proud grin on her face. "Like my system?"

I looked between her and the rope that extended out the window, imagining the bucket swinging over the street. "Genius."

Her grin widened. "I like to think so. They should notice it soon." She strode to the small door that led to the kitchen. "Want some wine?"

"Yes." The word burst from me, sounding a little too desperate.

Mac laughed. "Had a long day?"

"Let's just say I wanted more than tea when I met you earlier at your pub." I followed her into the little kitchen and accepted the glass of wine she handed me.

"What did you find out?" She handed me a glass of white wine, and I took it gratefully.

"He wants me to check the body for any missing organs." I explained the whole encounter, watching as her frown deepened. "I think maybe he didn't do it."

"Maybe he didn't. But that's weird, though—the missing organs. Does he think a necromancer is involved?"

I nearly choked on my wine. "Necromancer? Like, raising the dead?"

"And other death magic, yeah."

"Well, shit." Just the idea made my stomach turn.

Had Beatrix been killed by a necromancer? My eyes pricked with sudden tears.

"What wrong?" Mac asked.

"Um..." Should I tell her? I drew in a deep, uncertain breath. But I wanted to talk about Beatrix. "My best friend—only friend, really—was killed last year."

"Oh, no." Mac gripped my arm.

"I found her in an alley with her head bashed in. I was too late to save her, and—" I choked on a sob.

Mac pulled me into a tight hug, and something thawed inside me. I hugged her back, composing myself, then pulled away. "Anyway, I was too late. But she had a tiny spiral burn mark under her throat . . . the same mark that was on the dead guy I found."

"A necromancer's mark."

My gaze flashed up to her. "What?"

"Magic often leaves a mark. If she was killed in the name of necromancy, a mark would have been left on her skin."

"Oh, my God. Does that mean Beatrix is a . . . a . . ."

I faltered, unable to say it.

"A zombie?" Mac shook her head. "Not if you saw her body. That would be highly unusual. Something else about her death was used for the necromancer's magic."

"I did see it." My head spun. "So necromancers don't just bring back the dead?"

"No. They also use death in their magic."

I nodded, trying to make peace with it. "The Devil might also think it's a necromancer, then."

"He either saw the mark on the body, or he made one to throw you off the scent."

The necromancer might be a false lead? That meant the Devil might still be responsible. I struggled to believe it, but I had to consider everything. I remembered the feeling of him stalking me. He was a killer, there was no doubt. Whether he'd killed the guy in the alley was up for debate.

A shout sounded from the distance, and I realized it was coming through the living room.

Mac's face brightened. "That will be dinner!"

She hurried into the living room and leaned out the window "Thanks, Berat!"

When she hauled on the rope, the bucket appeared, and she grabbed it and brought it inside. Reaching in, she retrieved a stack of takeaway containers, all glass.

I eyed them, impressed and grateful for the distraction. "Fancy."

"Reusable." She grinned. "Better for the environment."

"You've got a good system worked out."

"It's the reason I'd never leave here. I don't even have to ring them to order my takeaway."

We settled down at the little table in the corner and dug in. The kebab was the best I'd ever had, and I swallowed with delight before talking. "Is there magic in this?"

"Probably." She shrugged. "It's not exactly legal—not here in Guild City, at least. But I think they've cut a deal with the Devil."

"The same Devil I just spoke to?"

"Yeah. That's the one. He's not government, but with the power he has, he might as well be."

"And the kebab place got his permission to put magic in the food? Like some special ingredient?"

"Yeah. The Council of Guilds—that's our actual government, by the way—restricts most magic use. But the Devil can get around their rules by convincing the right people of the right things. Or threatening them. And if you want to get around their rules, too, you pay him, and he makes it happen."

"So he's like some kind of criminal kingpin."

She shrugged again. "Basically. And maybe a murderer. Hopefully, Eve will finish that truth potion soon."

I leaned back in the chair, my stomach full. It should have made me content, but stress over the murder kept me on edge. "I need to sneak into the morgue. It's my only clue."

Mac nodded. "I'm wary of your source, but he's got a point. It's worth checking out."

I chewed on my lip. "Yeah, but how? I'm a wanted woman. My face will be all over the place."

"We need to make you unrecognizable."

"A makeover?"

"More like a disguise. Or invisibility, though that's harder."

"Does Eve have that stuff?" I was going to owe her a lot of favors.

"No. I mean, maybe she has some of it. But the people you really want to see are the witches."

"The ones I'm not supposed to get on the bad side of?"

"Same ones. But sometimes, we need their help."

"Can I trade them more favors?" I was throwing them around willy-nilly, but I needed to save my cash for living expenses, and somehow, it was easier to promise favors to be paid in the future. Maybe it was a bad idea, but it sure was easier. And why solve a problem today if I could solve it tomorrow?

"That's what they'll want, probably, yeah." Mac looked out the window, and I followed her gaze. The sun had set, and it was darker outside. "It's nearly the full moon. The witches will be having one of their masquerades tonight. We can sneak in, then try to sweet-talk them into helping us."

Helping us. Gratitude welled inside of me. "Thanks, Mac. Seriously, from the bottom of my heart."

"This is cool. And you're cool. I don't mind." With that, she surged to her feet and clapped her hands. "All right. We need to get dressed up!"

I stood, grinning at her. Damned if this wasn't cooler than my normal life.

8

The Devil

One by one, my muscles unfroze. The room was silent—the woman had been gone an hour, maybe more. Already, it felt like she had never been there. Her scent had left the air, along with the slight warmth she brought. The strangest sense of loss echoed through me, and I frowned.

Loss? Why the hell should I feel loss?

Why the hell should I feel anything at all?

But I did, and it was the oddest damn thing.

Irritation prickled over my skin. No one got the drop on me—not normally.

But she wasn't just anyone.

I'd been distracted. Nearly overwhelmed by the

animal instincts that I had worked so hard to repress.

She'd overwhelmed me.

I dragged a hand over my face. That hadn't happened in years. Centuries. Ever?

Disgust bubbled up within me. What was it about her? She was quick and clever. I couldn't control her. And it made me feel...things.

It was the most uncomfortable feeling.

I wanted to make it stop. To understand it, at least.

The woman—I needed to find her name. Find *her*.

I wanted to know more about her.

The potion bomb she'd thrown at me was familiar. I tasted the air, getting a hint of Eve's magic. She paid for protection from the witches, who would otherwise try to crush her small business.

I turned and strode toward the door, the thrill of the hunt already seething in my veins. *This*, I was familiar with. This, I liked.

The mirror near the door caught my reflection. Humans believed we couldn't be seen in mirrors, but my reflection proved otherwise.

For the briefest moment, I caught a glimpse of what the woman had seen. Cold eyes, pale skin, sharp fangs. I touched one briefly. For the shortest moment, I wondered what she'd thought of me. I lived a half life—one full of muted colors, tastes, and smells. Did she see the same monster that I did?

Or worse?

I shook the thought away and forced my fangs to retract, then turned toward the door. Finding her would be easy. I'd use all the contacts at my disposal, and they were vast. She was likely going to head to the human morgue to follow the clue I'd given her. But she might not have left Guild City yet.

As I marched down the hallway, I passed several of the cocktail waitresses. They skirted to the side to give me a wide berth, their movements twitchy and nervous. They were afraid of me. Almost everyone was afraid of me.

Once, I might have cared.

Now?

No.

It was unusual that I even noticed them unless I perceived a threat.

The club itself was quiet as I strode through. Midafternoon was one of the less busy times, which was fine. It was primarily a front for my main business, anyway.

I reached the hostess stand, and Miranda leaned toward me to tell me about the woman's escape. She'd frozen some of my guards, apparently.

Well done.

Fresh guards nodded as I emerged from the club and out into the watery sun. The light prickled against my skin but didn't burn like human movies suggested it would. Despite that, I stuck to the shadows as I made my way through Guild City. I was more comfortable there, even if the sun wouldn't incinerate me.

I passed a few citizens as I cut down the narrow alleys, and each one crossed the street to give me passage. They were even more afraid of me than my staff, though I didn't understand it. I didn't make a habit of killing people, after all.

I *did* kill people, of course. But not often. And not publicly.

Reputation could work wonders, though. And even I knew that I seemed icy. My past had followed me here, and people didn't forget easily.

Eve's shop was open when I arrived, and I entered silently. The tiny space smelled of a hundred different magics, all colliding with each other. I liked it in there because the sheer number of smells seemed to compensate for the fact that scent was always so muted for me.

Her wares cluttered the shelves, tiny bottles of potions gleaming in the dimness. Fairy lights sparkled near the ceiling of the shop. The raven sat on the shelf behind Eve, silent as always.

Eve glanced up, her expression bored. She froze when her gaze met mine, but she didn't so much as twitch—that is, except her arching right eyebrow, a clear question. She waited silently. I wondered how sure she was of my past. People whispered of it, but no one knew for sure.

Even I was uncertain after so many years. Visions all clashed in my mind.

I shook away the thoughts. "I'm looking for a woman. You sold her a freezing potion."

"Confidentiality."

"I'm sure there's a way around that."

She leaned back, crossing her arms over her chest. "There really isn't. Why are you interested in her?"

I didn't like the question. Partially because I didn't want to share, but also because I didn't want to examine it myself.

Why *was* I interested? Because something in me recognized her?

I shoved away the thought and sighed, more out of exhaustion than anything else.

She shifted nervously.

"Don't make me," I said.

She scowled. "I'm not making you do anything."

No, she wasn't. I chose to use my magic against her. Part of me didn't like it, but a bigger part wanted to find the woman.

I called on the power that had been given to me when I'd been made into a vampire so many hundreds of years ago. Most vampires were born. Turned vampires rarely survived the transition, and when they did, they woke up with insane bloodlust and muted senses, a mimicry of their previous lives. The combination led to them going on killing rampages that were so dangerous they often ended up dead themselves.

But somehow, I'd survived.

Magic swelled within me, dark and fierce, a vortex of power that reached out of me and into Eve. It was easier than it had been with the woman who'd just visited me. She had been impossible to influence.

Eve, however, was not.

She grimaced, her eyes shooting daggers at me.

My magical signatures flared on the air. It was something I normally kept a tight rein on, but I needed it now. I knew my signatures were horrifying. They'd served me well when I'd first been made. Screams of the dying, the icy grip of the reaper. The smell of brimstone and the taste of dirt.

She paled and shrank back, her bravado gone.

The worst I would do to her was force her to tell me what I wanted to know. Perhaps I could refuse to sell her my protection, but she didn't need to know that. I wouldn't waste time on killing her, not when the witches would jump to take out her shop. She was competition, and that Guild was fierce. I helped Eve stay open to irritate them.

"Tell me what I want to know. Who was the woman to whom you sold the potion?"

"Fine." Her words were tight, her eyes flashing with anger as my magic forced the truth from lips. "Her name was Carrow. She's some friend of Mac's, and she can read objects and people with a touch. That's all I know." She gave me a crafty smile. "And I just had my runner deliver a truth serum to her. So, be ready for that. She might even use it on *you*."

Interesting. "Thank you. If they visit you again, be sure to let me know."

She hissed at me, and I just smiled. "Good day."

If she responded, I didn't notice. My mind was already on the woman. Carrow. Her name was Carrow.

I strode out of the shop and turned toward Mac's door. She lived so close that it was worth checking.

What I would do when I found the woman…I wasn't quite sure. But I was curious, and I hadn't been curious in years. Finally, something interesting was happening.

The murder itself was only slightly noteworthy. True, I wanted to know who was behind it and what they were planning. Why they'd stolen the dagger from me. But it was Carrow herself who really piqued my interest.

At the green door that led to Mac's stairs, I used my city key. It opened almost any door in town and was a perk of having as much power as I did. Taking the stairs two at a time, I ascended silently. When I reached Mac's door on the second level, I knocked. I could have used the key like I had the bottom or even broken the lock, but a streak of conscience tugged at me. It was a rare and awkward feeling, quite frankly, but I heeded it. I definitely had a conscience; it was just well buried.

No one answered the door, and the space within was silent. My hearing was unnaturally good. No one was home. I turned and left, heading back toward my club. The bouncers waited at the front, still and silent. Both shifters had been in my employ for over a decade. Powerful and loyal, the best security was hired from the Shifters' Guild. Their eyes were cold and dead, but they weren't monsters.

Not like I was.

I passed them and stopped at Miranda's desk. My second in command leaned forward expectantly, a half smile on her face. She looked unassuming in her heels and simple black dress, but she could kill someone with a scream. One of the advantages of having a banshee on staff.

"Tell the city spies to let me know when they spot Mac and her friend," I said. "Immediately."

Miranda nodded. "Yes, sir."

I grinned, walking into the club.

If Carrow was in Guild City, she was mine.

Carrow

A couple hours later, after a catnap and a party makeover, Mac and I were dressed as fabulous postapocalyptic junkyard slum queens—colorful sequins and leather and platform boots. Eve's employee had delivered the truth serum, and I wore the tiny vial on a chain around my neck.

"This isn't my usual," I said as we strode down the streets of Guild City, magic sparking all around us. "But I like it."

"You look like a badass in your jeans and leather jacket," Mac said. "But this is a fun change."

"This whole thing is a fun change." The night was alive around us, the old buildings gleaming with light and magic. The interiors of the shop windows seemed to come alive.

All of this was so much better than my lonely flat and the constant doubt of the only people I knew. I missed Cordelia a bit, but she'd never paid me any attention, anyway, so she certainly wasn't missing me.

I turned my attention to the shops around me. *This* was what I was most interested in right now. My primary goal was to solve the murder, but I was going to have a small bit of fun while doing it. It was impossible not to stare at magic.

As we strode past a clothes shop, the outfits inside danced as if they were at a party we just had to join. Effective advertising, because it totally made me want a pair of really ugly jeans. They just looked like they were having such a good time.

The tea shop was giving the clothes shop a run for

its money, though. The kettles in the window were shooting colorful steam into the air, and the teabags were leaping like trained mice. Next door, swords clanged in a mock battle, and daggers shot around the empty store.

"This is so much cooler than my regular life." I could hear the wistfulness in my own voice.

"That bad, huh?"

I shrugged, dragging my eyes from a fishmonger's shop that seemed to be filled entirely with water. An octopus swam in fancy patterns, drawing hearts with ink that it shot from its back end. "It's fine. Just... normal."

"And you're not normal."

"I guess not."

Mac turned onto another street. Like all the rest, it was narrow and winding, with old buildings crowded together on either side. Most were in the Tudor style, made of white plaster and dark wood, with sharply slanted roofs and glittering mullioned windows. The shops here were quieter, but the stillness made it easier to hear the party in the distance.

"That's the witches," Mac said. "Their full moon masquerades are legendary."

"It's not the full moon, though." I looked up at the huge, glowing orb. We were probably a couple days away from full.

"They get excited and host it early." Mac shrugged.

"Only about once a year do they manage the restraint to wait until the moon is full."

I grinned, liking the witches already.

We turned at a bend in the street, and I could finally see all the way to the end. Colored lights exploded in the sky—like fireworks, just way too low to be safe. When we reached the end of the lane and I could get a better view across the square, I spotted a fantastic old tower that leaned slightly to the left.

Mac gestured to it. "Voila! The Witches' Guild."

"You're telling me." It was perfect.

I'd had no opinion about witches and their guilds before, but now that I saw this place…it looked just like it should. The tower itself was pale brown on a square base and teetered to the left like a drunk. Wooden staircases wrapped around the sides, leading up to a door. The windows were dark and empty, occasionally flashing with light.

And the roof…that was the best bit. Dark and pointed, like a witch's hat. Pale blue smoke wafted from a chimney, replaced occasionally with sparks of light. Music blared from the place, and I could feel the energy of the party inside. Every now and again, lights exploded right above the lawn—the fireworks that I'd thought I'd seen.

"Each guild tower is built right into the city wall," Mac said. "And each has a square in front of it."

I eyed the open space, which was covered in patchy

grass. The shops there were mostly derelict, run-down or closed.

"This part of town is shadier," Mac said. "You can blame the witches. They're so loud and destructive that shops don't want to risk it. This lawn catches fire at least twice a year, and spells shoot out the chimney all the time. Frankly, it's a hazard to be located close to them."

"The Council of Guilds doesn't control them?"

"They try. But it's hard. The witches are part of the council, so they've got some say."

"Sounds like they have a lot of clout."

"Yeah, that's what comes with powerful magic in Guild City, and the witches have some seriously powerful magic."

The moon peeked out from behind a cloud, bright and white. A wolf howled in the distance, and another one streaked across the lawn.

I stepped closer to Mac. "Was that a real werewolf?"

"Yeah. Some of them go nuts near the full moon."

"Will they…bite?"

"Nah. Not unless you want them to." She winked at me.

"No, thanks."

"Good choice." She laughed. "Let's go."

She strode across the lawn, and I followed. The music grew louder as we neared, and the lights flashing in the windows occasionally revealed people dancing.

"Is everyone in town invited?" I asked.

"No. And technically, we're not, either." She pulled her sequin mask down over her face. "But that's part of the fun."

We were going to gate-crash a masquerade held by witches.

Hell, yeah, that sounded fun.

Way more fun than my normal life.

Who'd have thought that getting accused of murder would be one of the best things to ever happen to me? Assuming I could clear my name and not get tossed in prison.

Mac took the creaky wooden stairs two at a time, and I followed her, pulling my mask down. It concealed the top half of my face, a glittery thing covered with sparkles that was more fabulous than anything I owned back in the real world. I hurried up the stairs in my platform boots. The heels were heavy, and I liked them. They would make a good weapon if I had to kick someone.

When we reached the front door, it swung open without us having to knock. A dour butler stood in the entry, his dark suit immaculately pressed and his white hair perfectly combed. He couldn't have looked less impressed if he tried, and I found myself loving him.

"Jeeves!" Mac grinned widely. "Long time no see, buddy."

"You are not invited, Macbeth O'Connell."

"Pshaw," Mac scoffed. "Check your list. You'll find my name."

Jeeves's white brows lowered. "I am certain I won't."

She touched his arm in a friendly gesture, her smile stretching wider. "I'm sure you wouldn't want Dorothea knowing about your little...hobby?"

Jeeves flushed scarlet, and I wondered who Dorothea was. My gaze moved to Mac's hand, where she still clutched at Jeeves. She was using her seer's gift on him and getting blackmail material, I realized.

Holy crap, that was dark.

And clever.

Jeeves sighed and stepped back. "You may enter. But no tricks."

"Tricks?" She pointed to herself. "Me? Never!"

He glared at her, and I followed her in, giving him an awkward little wave.

As soon as we entered, a crush of people surrounded us. Everyone was dressed to the nines, all in fabulous crazy outfits. There was a giant chicken who shot sparks out of its tail feathers, a monkey with golden fur, and an eight-legged dog who might have been an actual dog and not a costume.

"This place is wild," I murmured to Mac.

"No kidding." She grinned widely. "The witches know how to party."

"Do you gate-crash often?"

"Every time. It's part of the fun." She tugged on my arm. "Now come on, I've got something I need to do before we meet the witches. It'll only take half a second, but it's important. Then we're on to your stuff."

I followed her through the various rooms. Each was decorated differently, with fabulous furniture and wild art on the walls. It was all very haphazard and mismatched, but in a funky, cool way.

As we walked, I realized that the rooms were themed for the party. One was done up entirely in glowing red with a volcano in the corner. It went all the way to the top of the tall ceiling, spilling brilliant red lava. People danced around it, drunk and laughing, but I couldn't look away from the molten stream.

"Is that thing real?" I shouted to Mac over the noise. I knew it couldn't be, but it looked so lifelike, I had to ask.

"Yeah," she shouted. "Totally real!"

"Yikes." It defied the laws of science. But then, I'd entered a world of magic.

"Yeah, don't fall in. Someone dies at one of these parties at least once a year. Usually a drunken idiot."

Given the number of people dancing super-close to the river of lava that flowed through the room, I wasn't surprised. "This would never happen in the real world."

"The real world doesn't have magic out in the open like this," Mac said. "But then again, the Council of Guilds really doesn't like that the witches do this, either."

"How do they get away with it if the government

doesn't like it? I know they've got sway with the Council, but this seems over the top."

Mac turned to me and raised her brows. "Can't you guess?"

Of course. "The Devil of Darkvale."

"Exactly. He either uses his mind control power or threatens them."

I remembered the icy feeling of him. "My money is on threats."

"Mine, too." Mac turned back and kept pushing her way through the crowd.

We entered a Mardi Gras–themed room, complete with two massive floats and people on stilts. I squinted up at the performers towering over the chamber, admiring their feathery costumes in purple, yellow, and green. Gradually, it dawned on me that they weren't on stilts.

They were floating.

Man, I hadn't even had a drink yet.

In the next room, Mac muttered, "Bingo."

The room was themed like the moon, with rocky ground and dark walls. Gravity seemed to lessen here, and my steps were so light that I could bounce across the ground. "Holy crap, this is amazing!"

"Right?" Mac grinned back at me. "They've always got a low-gravity room like this at their parties. Last year, it was undersea themed."

"Nice."

"This way." She pulled me toward a table in the corner of the room against the wall. It was fairly normal looking, and I had a feeling it was here even when the room wasn't decorated and ensorcelled for the party. A bust of a regal woman sat on top of it, her patrician features staring in disapproval at the crowd.

"Who is that?" I asked.

"Hecate, one of their premier goddesses. I think they worship her or something." Mac pulled a vial of potion from her pocket and dumped it on Hecate's head.

The statue glowed briefly, then returned to normal.

"What was that for?" I asked.

"Every time I gate-crash a party, I play a prank on them. Then they play one back on me."

"What will happen?"

"When I say the magic words, Hecate here will start screeching, and she won't quit until they turn her off." She grinned widely. "It's fun for me, but it's also insurance."

"What kind?"

"The only way to shut her up is to get the password from me. If we get into a pickle breaking into your morgue, I say the magic words, and Hecate starts howling. When the witches call me, I'll demand their help in exchange for the password."

"Oh, genius." I held up my hand for a high five, and she smacked it.

"Come on," she said, "let's go find them."

9

CARROW

We bounced our way through the moon room and entered a tiki-themed space. A massive pool sat in the middle, and palm trees grew around the glittering blue water. There were half a dozen people in the pool, all standing around a floating table. Each end of the table had about a dozen red plastic cups sitting on it, each emitting colorful smoke.

Two women stood at either end of the table, tossing ping-pong balls at one another. When one of them landed a ball in her opponent's cup, the other woman had to drink.

"Holy crap." I leaned toward Mac. "Are they playing beer pong?"

"Potion pong. Much more dangerous."

The dark-haired woman on the left side of the table had green stripes through her hair and a bikini that glittered like black diamonds. She swigged back a cup of potion, then put it on the floating table. She grinned and shouted to the other woman, "That's all you've got?"

The blonde woman at the other side laughed. "Oh, just you wait, Coraline."

A half second later, Coraline grew a brilliant orange beak. Her masquerade mask shifted, and she chucked it off as she squawked loudly. It sounded something like, "Bitch!"

The blonde woman laughed like a loon.

"That's Mary," Mac whispered.

Coraline, still sporting her massive beak, picked up one of the small white balls and threw it at Mary's cup. It landed, and Mary grabbed it and slurped it back.

She shot out of the water, propelled by an unseen force, and landed in the top of one of the palm trees growing from the hardwood floor. She laughed hysterically, then jumped into the pool with an enormous splash, upsetting the beer pong table. The colorful potions in the red cups spilled into the water, sending purple and pink and green streaks bleeding outward.

Coraline's beak had disappeared, and she shouted. "Hey! No fair! I had some good potions there!"

Mary surfaced, her hair wet. "It's cool. We'll set them up again."

Coraline scowled at her. "You're ignoring the point."

Mary was about to respond, but her gaze landed on us. A huge smile lit up her face, and a shiver of unease went through me. It wasn't an entirely friendly smile, and when I looked at Mac, I realized that she had the same expression.

They were friends, but...

It was kind of a murdery friendship.

Mary waded over and hopped out of the pool. Her swimsuit was ridiculous, bright yellow with sopping yellow feathers and an eye over each breast. She was dressed like a slutty Big Bird, and I choked back a laugh.

"Mac! Have you pranked us?" she asked.

"You better believe it." Mac grinned. "But we need some help."

Mary crossed her arms over her chest and raised one eyebrow. "Oh?"

"Yeah." She nudged me. "My friend here can read the future and the past through objects. She'll trade you that for—"

"Nope!" Mary held up a hand. "She's got to play us in potion pong first, and if she survives, we can negotiate."

"Survives?" I asked.

Mary nodded. "We don't do business with just anyone."

"That's not true," Mac said. "You guys have basically no standards."

"Ha! We have weird standards, not *no* standards." She

gave me a look up and down. "And I can tell this one is trouble. Her aura screams it. So she's got to earn an audience."

"I can do it," I said. "In the pool?"

"Yeah." Mary grinned. "In a suit?"

"I don't have one."

"You do now." She waved her hands at me, and my glittery slum queen outfit disappeared, replaced by a bikini that was blue and fluffy.

I was the Cookie Monster.

Fantastic.

I touched the chain around my neck. At least I still had the truth serum.

"Come on." Mary hopped back in the water.

I looked at Mac.

"Good luck," she said. "If you can avoid drinking the potions, I would. If not…well, good luck."

"I'm going to grow a beak, aren't I?"

"You'll wish." She shook her head. "I think this will be a little tougher. Just try to keep your wits about you."

"Got it."

I strode toward the pool, watching as Mary and Coraline set up the potion pong table.

Coraline looked me up and down, studying me intensely from behind her pink mask. "I've hooked you up with some of my potions to make this fair."

"Thank you." I climbed into the water. It sparkled and bubbled against my skin. Colors swirled through it, and every time I walked through a cloud of pink or purple, the water seemed to tingle strangely.

The crowd cheered as I stepped up to the potion pong table.

A brief image of my lonely, lame flat flashed in my mind, along with the memory of how everyone in the London police force thought I was loony.

How the hell had my life changed so much?

Whatever, I was going to enjoy it.

As much as I could, at least. Mary's smile was making me uneasy. She looked like a cat who was about to play with a mouse...in a way that punctured a few of the mouse's vital organs.

I looked down at the red plastic cups full of potions. There were fifteen in front of me, all lined up to form a triangle. A ping-pong ball sat nestled against one of the cups, about to roll off the rocking table and into the water. I picked it up.

"I'll let you go first," Mary said.

"Get ready to have your ass kicked."

Mary laughed, sounding slightly crazed.

Oh, she was definitely getting her ass kicked. I aimed my ball and threw it, holding my breath as it sailed through the air and landed in one of her cups.

She groaned and tilted her head back, then picked up the potion and drank it.

Immediately, her head shrank to half its size, and

she screeched, the noise much higher pitched than it would normally be. "Coraline, you bitch!"

I laughed, and the sound drew Mary's attention. Despite her tiny head, I could see the murder in her eyes, and it was enough to shut me up. She squinted her little eyes and tossed the ball. It sailed through the air, landing in a cup full of gleaming black liquid.

Shit.

"Drink up!" Mary shouted.

I picked up the cup and fished out the ball, then slugged the potion back. It slithered down my throat, and I nearly gagged. The taste was a combo of old shoes and gummy bears, and I was damned certain I'd never eat another gummy bear ever again.

I set the cup down and gasped, trying to get control of my gag reflex. I wanted to puke.

I began to float instead, rising slowly out of the water.

"You still have to play your turn," Mary shouted. "If you fail, you lose!"

"Crap." I raised the little white ball and aimed. I was up to my knees now, way too aware that my crotch was at eye level with every person in the place.

Quickly, I chucked the ball.

It bounced off the table and landed in the water.

Mary laughed like a maniac and threw her ball. It landed in one of my cups, but I was floating too far above the water to reach the cup.

"You've got to drink it or you're out," Mary called.

I tried to swim through the air, but all I managed to do was point my ass to the sky. All around, people cheered.

At least it sounded friendly.

"Don't worry!" Mac shouted. "I've got you!"

She stood on the edge of the pool, holding the long handle of a pool net. I grabbed the rim of the net and used it to drag myself within reach of the cup Mary's ball had landed in. I raised the cup to my lips and chugged it, grimacing at the sour taste.

Immediately, gravity grabbed me again, and I plunged into the water with a splash. I shot upward, kicking as hard as I could. The pool water glittered blue and bright as I swam toward the air above. It took ages to reach the surface. Finally, my head broke through, and I gasped.

All around, people stared at me.

I blinked, looking up at them.

Why was I so short? And why had it taken so long to swim through a pool that was only waist deep?

I looked down at myself, seeing only a curved chest covered in feathers.

I squawked.

Holy crap, I'd turned into a duck!

"Play your turn, new girl," Mary shouted.

Oh, how I wanted to shit on her head. If I had to be a duck, that was the only pro I could think of to this whole situation. Instead, I honked angrily at her and awkwardly flapped my way out of the water.

It took all my concentration to fish my ball out of the cup with my beak. Flapping my wings awkwardly, I flew over and dropped the ball in Mary's cup.

She shrieked her rage, but Coraline shouted from the sidelines. "I call it good!"

Mary groaned, then reached for the potion.

Hell, yeah. Apparently, Coraline was the referee, and she was still annoyed with Mary. I flew back to my side and watched the blonde witch drink her potion. Steam poured out of her ears, and she shrieked like a teakettle.

A few moments later, I turned back into a human, and we kept playing. The game went fast, and fortunately, I didn't turn into any more birds. Finally, we were down to two cups. Whoever landed her ball first was going to win.

"Shoot at the same time!" Coraline shouted.

Okay, I could do that.

Only problem was, I felt utterly pissed. Something in the last potion made my head spin like a top. I blinked and squinted, gripping my ball too tightly and focusing on the one cup left in front of Mary.

"On the count of three!" Coraline shouted from the side. "Shoot!"

Shit, shit, shit!

I sucked in a deep breath, blinking frantically. I'd been drunk before. In fact, I used to have a tiny plastic basketball hoop on my fire escape that I'd found in the dumpster. I'd thrown a tennis ball in it over and over again, imagining that Cordelia was my cheering audience.

Sure, this red plastic cup was a hell of a lot smaller, but I could do this. I could *so* do this.

"One...two...three!"

Instinct and desperation took over. My life was on the line.

I tossed the ball, holding my breath as it flew through the air. Mary's ball shot toward me, and I wanted to knock it off track. I resisted, clenching my fists.

Finally, my ball dropped into her cup a split second before hers landed.

"Hell, yeah!" I raised my fists, victory surging through me.

Mary scowled. "I hate losing. But I kind of like you, so come on. Let's talk."

I looked at Mac. She raised her eyebrows and grinned, giving me a thumbs-up. I followed Mary to one end of the pool, wading through the water to the wide stairs. We climbed out, and she waved a hand at me. "Be dry."

My swimsuit immediately dried, and I grinned at her. "Thanks!"

"No problem." She gestured me toward a door. "Come on."

Coraline joined us, along with Mac and another girl with glowing dark skin and braids. A pigeon sat on her shoulder. The second room was shadowed and sparkly, the walls covered in glittery fabric. A disco ball hung from the ceiling. There was a padded leather booth in the corner that looked like something out of an old steak restaurant, and the rest of the room was filled with dancers.

A few women with tiny horns scrambled out of the booth as the witches approached. The three witches slid onto one side of the booth, still in their bikinis.

I was still in mine, for that matter, but I was drunk enough off Mary's magic that I couldn't complain.

Mac and I sat in the booth across from them. The girl that I didn't recognize leaned forward and grinned. "I'm Beth."

"Hi. Carrow."

"So I hear. And you want something from us."

"I'm willing to trade." I made my voice firm. Sure, this world was insane, and I felt totally outgunned by three witches, but I could at least pretend to hold my own. "I can read the history or future of objects. Sometimes people."

The three witches raised their brows.

"Pretty good," Coraline said.

"Pretty useful." Mary nodded.

"But what do you want from us?" Beth asked.

"A potion to change my appearance. Or better yet, to make us invisible."

Mary shook her head. "Nope, no can do on the invisibility. That shit takes forever to make and is, therefore, insanely expensive."

"You mean my magic isn't a worthy trade for an invisibility potion?" If I still had feathers, they would have ruffled.

Beth shrugged. "Don't know yet. Would rather sell you something easier and make sure your skills live up to what you're saying."

Fair enough, and it wasn't like I had time to wait for a complicated potion to be brewed. Time was ticking.

Jeeves appeared at the table, his back stiff and his lip curled with distaste as he looked at Mac. In his hands, he held a tray of silver goblets that emitted pink smoke.

"Jeeves!" Coraline shouted.

"Jeeves," the other two chorused.

I expected Jeeves to look irritated or long-suffering, but he seemed to glow with pleasure.

"Ladies." He set the platter on the surface of the table, and the three witches each leaned forward to grab a cup.

Mary whispered something to Jeeves that I couldn't hear.

Coraline eyed Mac and me. "Drink up, bitches!"

Mac and I grabbed a glass, and I took a sip. Flavor exploded on my tongue, the most amazing cocktail I'd ever had. I couldn't tell if it tasted like fruit or flowers or sugar or magic—probably all of the above. It was amazing, and I couldn't get enough.

Vaguely, I recognized that maybe I shouldn't be slugging it back like a two o'clock drunk, but I couldn't seem to help myself. My hand kept dumping the cocktail into my mouth, and I was all too happy to oblige.

Next to me, Mac did the same.

Finally, we finished and set our cups on the table.

Mac shook her head and looked down at the cup, then up at the witches.

"Holy crap." She scowled. "You put ambrosia in that."

"Sure did." Beth cackled.

"What's ambrosia?" My voice nearly slurred.

"Witchy drugs," Mac said. "We'll be high off our asses soon."

"Godly drugs," Coraline said. "And they're hard to come by." She beamed. "You're welcome."

"Thank you." Maybe I shouldn't have been thanking them, but everything seemed so nice right then.

It took every inch of willpower to drag my attention back to the witches and my reason for being there. I leaned on the table and stared hard at them. "Okay, what about that potion?"

"Sure," Coraline said. "We can do that. But first, you have to tell us why you want it."

"I'm wanted for murder."

All three witches sat back, brows raised and mouths pursed. I was ninety-nine percent sure it was an expression of respect.

"Nice," Beth said.

Yep, it was respect.

Weirdos.

"How'd you do it?" Coraline grinned, which looked more like a bloodthirsty grimace.

"We're assuming the dude deserved it," Mary said. "Nothing like murder to teach a person a lesson."

Well, that was true.

I *so* did not want to get on the bad side of these witches.

"I didn't actually do it," I said.

All three witches slumped and scowled.

"Boring," Mary said.

"Holy crap, you guys are intense," I muttered.

"She's from the human world." Mac leaned toward the witches, her tone apologetic. "They don't have tons of demons and other bastards running around who need killing."

"Sure, we do," I said. "Not the demons part. But there are loads of bastards. Not sure about the killing part, though."

"It's different in this world," Mac said. "There are lots of nasty humans, sure. But supernaturals are a whole 'nother breed. Demons, for instance. Lots of them like to eat babies. Gotta kill those ones."

"You can chop their heads off and they'll just wake up back in hell," Beth said. "And don't get me started on black magic users. Some of them are so evil that hell won't even take them."

"Okay, well…" My mind raced as I tried to figure out what to say to get in the good graces of these witches. It was hard with the potion surging through my veins, but I slogged through and said, "I'd definitely kill those suckers."

All three witches grinned.

Mary leaned back. "All right, then. So, you didn't kill this bloke back in your realm, but you're accused of the murder and you're…wanting to prove your innocence?"

"Exactly!" I pointed at her approvingly. "You get it!"

"It's not rocket science, honey."

"Everything after one of those cocktails feels like rocket science."

"Fair enough," Beth said.

"I need to be able to sneak into the morgue," I explained.

"And I need to go with her," said Mac.

Coraline nodded. "Okay. Two potions to change your looks."

"I don't know if I need one," Mac replied. "They won't recognize me in the human world."

"Well, you're getting one because we have two objects we want read."

"Deal," I said. "I can do that when I get back."

"Now," Coraline insisted.

Her tone was firm, and I nodded. "Sure thing, boss."

Jeeves appeared again, a box in his hands. He looked at Mary as he set it on the table. "The things you requested, madam."

"Thanks, pal." Mary slapped him on the back as he walked away, then pushed the box toward me. The grin she shot me made a shiver go down my spine, and I stared at the box like there might be a head inside.

10

CARROW

"That was quick," I said.

"That's me, mate." Mary nodded to the box. "Now get reading."

I opened it slowly, revealing an old wine glass and an intricate silver brooch. I stared at them before touching. "I can't control if I see past or present. But usually, what I see is useful."

"Useful how?" Mary asked.

"It reveals when danger is coming, or when something terrible happened. Sometimes good stuff, too, but that's rare."

"Well, try to see who once owned them."

"I'll try." True, my vision was currently blurry, and I

felt like I might keel over on the bench soon, but maybe this would help.

I drew in a deep breath and tried to imagine seeing the original owner. I had no idea if this was how magic worked, but I figured I might as well try.

"Show me the owner," I murmured, feeling like a crazy witch in an old movie.

I glanced up at the three actual crazy witches in front of me, then down at the Cookie Monster bikini I was wearing. *Hmm...not so far off the crazy witch vibe, myself.*

My fingers closed around the wine glass, and an image slammed into my head. A beautiful blonde woman dressed in some kind of old-fashioned clothing, like something from a World War II movie. Same for her precise makeup and sculpted updo. I could vaguely hear another person speaking in the background of the vision: "I told you I'd curse you, Ophelia."

Ophelia?

A shadow appeared from the side, bringing with it a flash of pink light that enveloped Ophelia. Chanting sounded in a language that I didn't recognize, and I struggled to memorize the words. Ophelia shrieked, then shrank into a tiny silver brooch.

I blinked, looking at the brooch that still sat in the box.

It was the same.

I jerked back, shock lancing through me.

"What is it?" Mary's voice interrupted my vision.

I looked up. "Uh, I think this brooch might be a person."

"Told you." Mary nudged Coraline. "What else did you see, Carrow?"

I described the pink smoke and the words that the person had said, hoping I got them right. The witches seemed satisfied, at least from the looks on their faces.

"Do the brooch now," Mary said.

I touched the brooch, which burned like hell. Blackness exploded in front of my vision, and I surged backward.

"Shit." Shaking my hand, I looked up. "I couldn't see anything besides darkness."

"Well, that Ophelia is a bitch."

"And she's now a brooch?" I looked down at the metal.

"Yeah, and we've got to get her out," Beth said.

"I thought you said she was a bitch," I said.

"Yeah, she's *our* bitch." Coraline grinned. "What exactly did you see in the brooch?"

"Blackness, like I said. Let me try again."

I touched it once more, and a shrieking sounded, followed by a bright flash of light in the shape of three triangles overlapping each other. I opened my eyes and described it to them.

Mary nodded. "Thanks for your service. You've

confirmed what we thought and told us the spell that turned her into that thing."

I didn't remember telling them a spell, but they seemed satisfied. "No problem."

"Jeeves will bring you the potions to change your appearance." Mary looked at Mac. "You *both* need to take them."

"In the meantime, enjoy the party." Beth grinned.

"We kind of need to get a move on," I said, my head still woozy.

"Well, you're going to need to walk off your drunk a bit," Coraline said. "Might as well do it here."

"Yeah, sure." I looked at Mac, who nodded.

The three witches left, hurrying off with their box. Which contained their friend.

Weird.

Mac looked at me. "I'm going to go try to find something so we can sober up some."

"Cool." I turned and looked at the glittering room. People still danced, seeming to sway in front of my vision. A flash of movement in the corner caught my eye, and I blinked. "What was that?"

"What?" Mac asked.

"I swear I saw something."

Mac frowned. "You're pissed."

"Maybe. But I saw something."

"Go investigate. I'll find you soon."

"Deal." I staggered toward the flicker of movement

against the dark, glittering wall. My steps became more graceful the farther I walked, but I was still pretty out of my mind. Fortunately, the drunken dancers around me hid most of my awkwardness.

As I neared the wall, the air seemed to vibrate slightly. I pushed my way through the rest of the crowd, finding a hallway. It was shadowed and apparently empty, but it beckoned to me.

My heartbeat surged as I stepped toward it.

Was someone in there?

I moved forward, swaying only slightly now. I still felt drunk, but I at least had control of my limbs. I wasn't going to faceplant.

Anticipation surged through me as I stepped into the darkened hallway.

I smelled him before I saw him—a spicy, whiskey-and-fireside scent. And the connection...that strange fizzing in my chest, a lightness I'd never felt before. The wire that connected us.

The Devil of Darkvale was here.

I squinted into the dark, barely able to make out the shadow of a man. He was huge, towering over me with a leonine grace that was all threat. My heart leapt into my throat as my hand flashed out and miraculously collided with a light switch. I flipped it on, and a faint golden glow gleamed from the ceiling.

It cast the Devil in a fiery light that only seemed to emphasize his icy hardness. He leaned casually against the wall, every muscle perfectly still but ready to pounce. If I tried to run, he'd be on me in a heartbeat.

Shadows flickered over his eerily perfect features, making his cheekbones look sharp as glass and his lips full and kissable. They didn't fit with the rest of his hard face, and the contrast made something in my belly flutter.

He was still dressed in an impeccable suit, but it didn't make him look staid or boring or even like a businessman. No, he looked like a spy. If spies had fangs. I couldn't see his now, but the memory of them flickered in my mind.

"Why are you here?" I was glad that my voice sounded stable. I could still feel the wooziness that came with the drink I'd had earlier, but the sight of him sobered me up some.

His gaze traveled down my body, and I remembered with a start that I was still dressed in the blue bikini. My hair was wet.

We were a good two meters apart, but it was too close. I stepped back.

"Nervous?" he asked.

"When you look at me like I'm a piece of steak, yeah."

"Not steak."

"No?"

"Cake."

I scowled at him. "I am not food." I pointed to his

mouth. "And considering the fact that you *do* eat people, I'm finding that comparison a bit too close for comfort."

Something unidentifiable crossed his handsome face. "I don't eat people."

"Hmm, I feel like you're splitting hairs." I kept my distance. "Why are you here?"

"I followed you."

"Yeah, that's what I was worried about. Why?"

"You froze me in my own office."

"You scared me."

"I did?" He raised an eyebrow.

"Yeah." I shifted, wishing I had a weapon on me. It was weird to be attracted to someone I was terrified of.

"Do you scare easily?"

"Only when it's wise."

"Is it wise now?"

Something tingled down my spine, and I wondered. "Undetermined. Why are you here?"

"I'm interested in you."

You. Not the murder, but *you.*

Maybe because he was the murderer. I couldn't rule it out, even though it seemed less likely. At least, it *felt* less likely. I hoped my attraction wasn't driving me off the scent.

Nerves shivered up my spine. "Oh?"

An unseen force seemed to tug me toward him, and I resisted it. I wanted to get close enough to touch him, but I also wanted to walk out of here with all my fingers intact. Not to mention my throat.

I reached for the vial hanging around my neck, unscrewed it from the chain., and held it up. "This is a truth serum from Eve. Drink it and tell me you didn't commit this murder *or* the murder of a woman killed on Fleet Street on the twentieth of June last year."

His gaze moved between the little bottle and me. "Fine."

My heart thundered. He took the vial from me, his touch avoiding mine.

In the flash of an eye, the potion was gone. "I didn't murder either of those people."

The words flowed easily from his lips, and the slightest bit of tension left my body.

"Who was the woman."?" he asked.

"A similar victim."

"With a necromancer's mark?"

"Yes." I looked to the left of him.

"Why won't you look me in the eye?" he asked.

"I've heard about your power to control people."

"I don't need eye contact for it to work."

I frowned. "You haven't tried it on me, then?"

"In fact, I have." His hand moved toward my face, and I froze solid.

Gently, his fingertips rested against my chin. The slightest pressure moved my head. Suddenly, I was looking right at him, unable to drag my gaze away from his icy eyes. It seemed like heat flickered in their depths, but that couldn't be right. He was an ice-cold statue, no matter how much he heated me up inside. I'd never thought I had a death wish, but my interest in this guy suggested I had a big one.

"I'm really immune to you?" I asked.

"It seems that way."

"And that's…rare?"

"Exceedingly." Interest rang in his voice.

I wanted to know more about him. And that required touching. The contact between my face and his hand didn't count. I needed to lay my own hand upon him.

I drew in a deep breath and slid closer, hoping he wouldn't notice. His gaze sharpened as he watched me.

"Do you want to use your power on me?" he asked.

"You know about that?"

"I know everything."

"Hardly."

"I do."

"What's my favorite ice cream?"

"Everything that matters."

"Oh, that matters." I inched forward a bit under the guise of leaning against the wall.

He held out his hand, palm up. "I know what you want. Go ahead."

I glared at him, not liking that I was transparent. I was also wearing about twelve square inches of fabric right now, so it wasn't like I had any secrets here. And I wanted to know his secrets.

Quick as a snake, I shot my hand out and gripped his.

Heat surged up my arm, suffusing me with warmth. Attraction tightened in my lower belly, and a shiver ran over me.

But there was no information to be had.

I blinked up at him. "There's nothing."

"Really?"

"This can't be right. My power always works." It might not show me what I wanted to see, but it always showed me *something*. I tried not to focus on the place where our palms still met. Awareness buzzed through me, so intense that it made my head spin. I didn't know if I wanted to run away or throw myself at him.

Both.

Visions of us in bed together flashed in my mind, but it was just my imagination. In fact, my imagination was pretty damned stellar at conjuring visions of him naked. Lots of lean muscle and eager hands and a hot mouth.

Whoa, girl.

I jerked my hand back, shocked.

That was all my imagination. Right?

"Done so soon?" he asked, his voice smooth.

Gasping slightly, I tried to get it together. I was just drunk, that was all. And I should be using this opportunity to grill him for more information if I couldn't read it from a touch.

But what did it mean, the fact that our powers didn't work on each other?

"Why are you so interested in this murder?" I asked. "That is, if you aren't the murderer."

"Would you be standing in a darkened hallway with a murderer?"

"I've done worse. And I can protect myself."

"Without a weapon? Without shoes, even?"

Yeah, he had a point. I was woefully underprepared. I could blame the witches and their potions all I wanted, but I'd gotten myself in here.

I stepped back. "Well? Why are you so interested?"

"Carrow?" Mac's voice sounded from the room outside the hall. I turned to look for her and saw her enter the hallway with a confused frown. "What are you doing back here alone?" she asked.

"Alone?" I turned back to the Devil, but he was gone. "Shit. That bastard."

"What bastard?"

"The Devil of Darkvale came here."

Mac laughed like I was crazy. "That ambrosia hit you hard."

"No, I swear it." I turned to her, heart pounding. "I know he was here. I saw him."

Mac's brows rose. "Really?"

"Yeah."

"Wow. That's unusual."

"He doesn't normally come to this party?"

She laughed again. "He doesn't socialize at all. Honestly, I don't know what he does in the evenings. Torture people for fun?"

"If he really was Vlad the Impaler, then maybe." The thought made me shiver. If history was anything to go by, Vlad had done horrible things. If he was truly a vampire, then those horrors could have been multiplied tenfold.

And if the Devil really was that man, then I didn't want his interest at all.

Liar.

"He came here for you?" Mac sounded nervous.

"He said he was interested in me. And I got confirmation that his power doesn't work on me. And that he didn't commit the murders."

"He took Eve's potion?"

"Yep."

Mac whistled low. "Well, try to avoid him if you can, anyway."

I nodded. It was the best idea I'd heard all day, even as part of me screamed to get closer to him. "Ready to go?"

"Yeah. Jeeves gave me the potions to change our faces. And I got some stuff to sober us up." She shoved a glass at me. "Drink that. You'll feel normal in no time."

I swigged it back as she drank her own.

"Let's get out of here," she said. "It's nearly dawn."

"What?" Shock lanced me.

"Time flies at the Witches' Guild."

"No kidding." Exhaustion tugging at me, I followed her from the house. As we walked through the pool room, I passed Coraline and pointed to the bikini I still wore. "Can you put me back to normal here, please?"

"Fine." She gave me an up and down look. "But you look better like that."

"Thanks, but no thanks. My own clothes, please."

"If you insist on those abominations." She waved her hand at me, and my clothes reappeared on my body, replacing the bikini.

"Thank you."

"No problem, babe. Come on back anytime. We like you."

A bit of warmth flared to life inside me. More possible friends? The witches were kind of iffy, but that was cool.

Not to mention the magic. That part, I certainly didn't hate. It filled the air here, sparking off people as they partied and drank.

Though it was almost dawn, the party was still heaving. People danced, so many of them that the crush of bodies was nearly impossible to navigate. All around, revelers with horns and fangs and wings danced the night away, living their best life. Like it was normal that they existed.

Which it was.

Thank God it was.

My life had been in black and white, and now it finally felt like it was in color.

We were almost to the foyer when a hand grabbed my arm, pulling me to a stop. I spun around, instinct making me ready to lash out.

A small woman held me, her grip shockingly strong for someone her size. Her face seemed to flicker between age and youth, a shimmery apparition that was hard to focus on. She was beautiful in either version—I just wanted her to pick one.

Her eyes burned with pale fire as she stared hard at me, her brow creased. I felt Mac appear at my side, but I couldn't turn away. The woman's gaze had me snared.

The crowd parted to give us space. No one turned to watch us, but there was something about the woman's presence that made them give her a wide berth.

"Yes," she said softly. "You are as I expected."

"What?" I frowned down at her.

"You are the one who will thaw him."

"Thaw who?"

"She's not a Fire Mage," Mac said.

The woman ignored her, leaning up to peer more closely into my eyes. "Be wary, girl. You are bound to the Devil, and you may grow to like it, but there is danger there. Grave danger."

"Bound?" Was she talking about the Devil of Darkvale?

"Like, Fated Mates?" Mac demanded. "Impossible."

"Yes, impossible," the woman said. "Turned vampires do not have Fated Mates like born vampires do. But turned vampires like the Devil—the immortal ones—have Cursed Mates. Beware. It could cost you your life."

"What the heck?" *Cursed mates?*

The woman let go of my arm and disappeared.

Like, really disappeared, right into thin air.

Shit, shit, shit. I didn't like any of this. I didn't understand it. And I didn't want to believe it.

But there was no denying everything I'd seen in the last twenty-four hours. Magic was real, and it had me in its grip.

I looked up at Mac. "Cursed mates?"

"Never heard of it."

I shrugged I off, not liking the sound of it. "Who the hell was that, anyway?"

"We call her the Oracle, but no one knows for certain. She's the most powerful seer in the city—way more powerful than me. She's lived here for centuries."

"Yeah, her face was..." I waved my hand in front of my own and made an expression that suggested *nuts*.

"I don't know what that is, either. But let's get out of here." She tugged my arm, and I followed her, head spinning.

Mac and I pushed our way through the crowd, approaching Jeeves, who stood with the door already open. The frown on his face was dour as he looked at the two of us, and I could already hear him saying, "Good riddance," as he shut the door on our retreating backs.

"Toodles, Jeeves, my love." Mac wiggled her fingers in his face as she sailed by.

"Thanks," I said, following her into the predawn.

The air was crisp and fresh, but still, heat seemed to suffuse me. I turned back to look at the tower.

Was the Devil watching?

It sure felt like he was.

11

Carrow

Mac and I hurried down the creaky wooden stairs of the Witches' Guild, the sound of the party following us across the lawn. I glanced behind again, half-expecting to see the Devil of Darkvale staring after me.

He'd come to the party just for me.

But he wasn't standing there. And neither was Jeeves. The door was shut, but the party was still making the leaning wooden building shake.

I turned back and hurried along with Mac, the early dawn sun beginning to turn the sky a light gray.

I liked Mac. I *really* liked having her help through this magical new world. But there was no fooling myself.

I was alone in this. I had always been alone, and I always would be.

I shook away the negative thoughts—they were total bull—and stepped onto one of the narrow streets that led back toward her place.

Wait, *was* that where we were headed?

Exhaustion pulled at me, and I looked at Mac. "Do you mind if I crash on your couch for a few hours? I'm beat, and I don't think we should try to sneak into the morgue in broad daylight. Too many people."

She nodded. "Of course. Where else would you go?"

"There?" I pointed to a little wrought iron bench that sat in front of a shop selling enchanted witches' hats of all styles and colors. "Unless there's a hotel around forty pounds a night. Because that's all I've got."

"Yeah, you're on my couch. Don't worry about it."

"Thank you." I couldn't believe my luck in finding someone like Mac to help me. I was going to need to pay her back big time.

As we neared her flat, I began to feel someone watching me.

The Devil?

No. His attention had a weight that made me prickle with anticipation and wariness.

This...wasn't like that.

It felt almost like family.

I looked around the old street, which was dead silent

in the hour before dawn. It was empty save for a few purple pigeons and the motion behind the shop windows—cauldrons bubbling away, enchanted clothing dancing, and quills writing on scrolls like their feathers were on fire.

Finally, my gaze landed on two small green eyes high against a building. There, on a ledge, sat a raccoon.

"Cordelia?"

Mac looked at me. "Who the heck is Cordelia?"

"That raccoon." I pointed to the furry little creature.

"You sure? Did it tell you its name?"

"No. I—" I paused. This was nuts. "Forget it. I'm going crazy."

"We all are, honey." Mac rubbed my arm. "Don't worry about it."

Cordelia stared down at me, the weight of her gaze heavy. Then she disappeared, jumping down into an alley and losing herself amongst the shadows.

Strange.

Mac led us to her flat and got me set up on the couch. As soon as I lay down, my whole body seemed to melt. "Thank you so much."

"No problem." She disappeared into her room, shouting out, "See you in the afternoon. Then we can make our game plan for the morgue."

"Good deal." I closed my eyes, listening to the sounds of the city waking up. The window was open, emitting a nice breeze and the smell of coffee from somewhere on the street down below.

~

I dreamed of the murder. Of meeting the Devil of Darkvale. Of the raccoon who I'd sworn was Cordelia. She had visited me, sleeping on my stomach as I slept on the couch.

Eventually, my mobile woke me, buzzing like mad next to my head on the pillow. I jerked upright, panting, and looked at it.

A text from Corrigan.

Shit.

Memories of every horrible thing I was trying to fight flashed in my mind. The murder. The manhunt.

I opened the message.

The entire police force is looking for you. Your face is on posters in shop windows. Turn yourself in.

Shit, shit, shit. That was *intense.*

It was ramping up to be a real serial killer investigation—and I was the main suspect.

"Breakfast," Mac sang out from the kitchen.

I jerked, turning toward the kitchen door. She

stepped out, carrying a tray with two big glasses of milk and a familiar blue package.

"Oreos for breakfast?" I asked.

"With milk!" She grinned widely. "That's how it's healthy."

"Of course." Despite the warning from Corrigan, a smile spread across my face. "Can't imagine a better breakfast.

"Me, neither."

We ate the Oreos quickly, cutting through almost half the package.

"So, ready to go sneak into the morgue?" Mac asked.

"Yeah. Can we pay a visit to Eve first, though?" Now that magic was an option, I wanted to use it. I had a lot of skills, but breaking and entering wasn't one of them. Especially not when the building in question was guarded like the morgue. I was willing to rack up some debts with Eve to improve my chances of getting in.

"Sure thing. She should be open."

Thankfully, it turned out she was. The shop looked the same as it had when we'd entered the first time—cluttered and full of magic, the potion bottles jammed onto the walls and faerie lights in the ceiling—but Eve looked different.

She looked guilty.

Hell, she almost grimaced when she looked at us.

"What's wrong?" Mac demanded at once.

"The Devil got to me," Eve said. Behind her, the raven twitched in irritation.

"Damn it." Mac looked between Eve and me. "What did he want to know?"

"He forced you to do something?" I asked, my mind racing with horrible ideas.

"He wanted answers."

"About what?" Mac asked.

"About her." Eve nodded at me. "Her name, what she does. Anything I knew."

"Is that how he found us at the party last night?" I asked.

She shook her head. "I didn't know that, so he probably found that info somewhere else. But I did tell him your name and what you can do. I tried to fight it, but I couldn't.

Mac shook her head. "Don't worry about it, Eve. *No one* can help it. That's the point of his power."

I didn't mention that *I* could help it. But I also didn't blame Eve. I'd felt the strength of his magic last night after the potion pong game. It would be impossible to resist.

"Well, I'm sorry," Eve said. "Probably better if you don't tell me anything."

"Can we ask for help, though?" I asked.

"Definitely." Eve's shoulders seemed to sag with relief. "I would be *delighted*. I feel like I owe you."

"You don't." I shook my head. "From what I understand, the Devil's ability to force people to do his bidding is part of life here."

In fact, it seemed that he was so powerful, he basically owned this city. No one could move without him knowing it. I shivered, wondering if this place was even more dangerous than London.

"You're telling me." A cloud crossed Eve's face. "But what can I help you with? And keep the details to a minimum. I don't want the Devil getting your info out of me."

"Okay…" He knew what I was going to try to do, but it'd be best to play by her rules anyway. "Do you have anything that will force people to do what I want them to do?"

"You want a power like the Devil's, huh?"

"Wouldn't be bad."

"True enough, it wouldn't." She went to a shelf and got down a small vial. "This is a powder that will make someone perform a small task for you. Nothing too intense, of course. You couldn't compel someone to kill, for instance."

My brows popped up. "Whoa, wasn't thinking of that as an option, actually."

"Okay, good. Well, it should work pretty well at getting someone to do something small, then. But they'll pass out immediately after."

"It won't hurt them, right?"

"No, it will exhaust them."

"That's fine. What about another freezing potion?" Mac asked. "That would be handy."

"You can have two. What else?"

Mac's eyes widened. "Wow, you really feel guilty, huh?"

"Yeah. Way guilty. He...he has his eye on her in a big way, and I don't know why."

"It's fine." I wanted to reassure her. "I can handle it."

"Against the Devil himself?" Eve looked skeptical.

"Against anything."

She grinned. "I like you. We should get a drink when this is all over, whatever this is."

"Yeah." *Two* friends? How could I get so lucky?

She gave us a couple more assorted potions that Mac seemed pleased with. We made sure that we were immune to the freezing potions, and then we split, heading back toward the gate.

The town was bustling by now, the sun setting once again. The old iron streetlamps and shop windows glowed with golden light, and the streets were full of supernaturals going about their business. A few people flew overhead, their wings carrying them through the air.

"I can't believe this place," I murmured.

"Well, get used to it. These are your people now."

I spotted two inebriated men brawling, horns protruding from their heads and drunken eyes rolling as they tried unsuccessfully to land a punch.

"Uhhh..." I said.

"Not those old goats. They're not your people." She pointed to some laughing women who looked mostly normal as they sat at an outdoor cafe drinking wine. "They are. Or maybe the old dudes playing cribbage over there." She laughed.

"You know, I'm not bad at cribbage."

"Maybe you can give old Larry and Watson a run for their money one day."

"I'd like to try."

As we passed through the main city gate and walked down the darkened tunnel to the other side, I felt a prickle of attention that made my heart race.

The Devil was watching. I could feel it in my soul, in the way the gaze felt like a caress over my skin.

"Can the Devil see inside here?" I asked.

"It's safe to assume he can see almost anywhere," Mac said. "Either through magic or through a secret hiding place. That man has eyes everywhere."

I rubbed the back of my neck uncomfortably. "Cool, cool, cool."

We reached the other side, and when we stepped out into the light, the ether pulled me in and spun me through space. A moment later, we appeared in the empty, darkened hallway of the Haunted Hound.

Quinn, the handsome bartender, stood near the shelves of liquor, adding another bottle. He looked at us, and his brows rose. "Come to cover your shift, Mac?"

"Ah, no. Can you?"

His eyebrows lowered, but his glower did nothing to obscure his handsome face.

"I'm helping Carrow," Mac said.

Quinn's face cleared again, and he seemed to be considering. "I could help Carrow. Be delighted to."

"You don't know what we're doing. She'd be better off with me."

"I'm not so sure of that."

"We're going to get our hair done."

He scowled. "Liar. But I'll still cover for you."

"Thanks a million," Mac said. "You're a hero."

"Seriously," I added. "Thank you. I could really use the help."

"Need a second person?" Quinn asked.

"We've got it," Mac said with a grin. "You'll have to flirt with her later."

"I'll count down the hours," he replied, charming as hell.

Unfortunately, it didn't do much for me. Sure, he was hot and nice, but he was no scary vampire with mind control. Which seemed to be the only guy I was interested in right now, which was insane, because I was also freaking scared of him.

"Actually," Mac said. "We could maybe use some bailout help later."

"Bailout help?" I asked.

"Hopefully not. But there's no point having friends if

they can't bail you out of trouble."

"What are you up to?" Quinn asked.

"Breaking into the city morgue," I said.

"And if we get in trouble, we might call you," Mac said. "We've already got the witches as an option, but they're unreliable. You're not."

"That's true. But why are you giving me a heads-up? Normally, you wait until you're up shit creek to ask for a paddle."

"Because we're going to look different." Mac dug into her pocket and held up two little potion bottles. "And we need you to know which two damsels to come rescue."

"You've never been a damsel."

"Damn right I haven't." She grinned.

She handed me a tiny vial of potion. "This one is for you. Specially formulated by the witches."

"Thanks." It was warm in my hand—unusually so.

"Same time?"

"Yep." I uncorked the vial and raised it, waiting for Mac.

Together, we swigged them back. Mine tasted disgustingly sweet and syrupy, and a shiver went through my whole body, followed quickly by a shaft of pain. I doubled over, the pain turning to agony.

Were the witches trying to kill me?

Mac groaned and nearly collapsed.

Scratch that, they were trying to kill both of us.

As suddenly as it had arrived, the pain departed. I gasped and stood. Mac did the same, and I gasped.

Quinn started to chuckle, his gaze moving between the two of us.

Mac looked different. Like, way different.

And not in a good way.

In fact, she reminded me of a toad—green skin and all. The only good part was that she was still standing on two legs and not four.

"Wow, you're hot!" Mac said.

"What?" I asked.

"Yeah. Totally hot. What do I look like?"

"Uh..."

"Come on," Quinn said. "There's a mirror behind the bar."

We followed him out. The place was half full, but no one paid us any mind.

Well, that wasn't quite true. There were some looks, a few cringes, but they didn't point and laugh, so I considered it a win. Apparently, frog girls were normal in the Haunted Hound.

We reached the mirror and gazed at our reflections.

Mac screeched with indignation. "Those bitches!"

Holy crap, I *did* look hot. Like, hot in a men's magazine kind of way. Wavy auburn hair and an impossibly perfect face, complete with impeccable makeup.

"I can't believe they did this," Mac muttered, rubbing at her green skin.

"This is one of their pranks, isn't it?"

"Yeah." She glowered. "And I'm going to get them for it."

"Man, we're going to draw some attention."

"No kidding." She dragged a gnarled hand over her face. "This is almost worse. We don't even look like real people."

Quinn looked between the two of us, seemingly delighted by the drama playing out in front of him.

"I look kind of real," I said.

"No, you don't, honey. No one looks like you in real life. You look like you've been photoshopped. You should see your waist. You're basically a Barbie doll."

I looked down, surprised to see that she was right. I should be wearing a corset to get a waist like this. And did my feet look pointed? Like I should be perpetually forced into tiny plastic heels?

I tugged up my hood, shoving the mass of red underneath.

"You've got to give me five minutes," Mac said. "I need a hood, too."

"Okay."

She hurried toward the hallway to go back to Guild City.

"Can I get you something, Miss January?" Quinn asked.

I shot him a look and gestured to my new Barbie body. "Oh, you like this, do you?"

"Actually, I prefer the real you." He leaned over the bar and shot me a charming grin. "A lot. So, when you're back to normal, if you'd like to get dinner or something, I'd be delighted to be your Ken."

I didn't want him, but I did like him. And warmth suffused me at his words. "Thanks. But I think...well, I'm going to have a lot on my plate."

"That's okay." He winked. "I'll try again later."

Mac returned a moment later with a hoodie. She tore the tag off it and tugged the garment over her head. Suddenly, her face was cast in shadows, nearly impossible to see. I could get glimpses of her, and she still looked like hell, but the magic in the hoodie seemed to soften her features, making them hazy. Her green skin looked slightly sallow now, and she only sort of resembled a frog.

"What's up with that hoodie?" I asked.

"Magic. I still look like me—or like Frog Me—but the hoodie makes it hard to get a good look."

"We should have just bought some of those."

"No. If you can be recognized, they'd still recognize you if they looked for a few seconds." She glowered. "Me, though. I tried to tell them I didn't need a potion."

"They just wanted to turn you into a frog," Mac said. "Joke's on them, though. You make a hot frog."

She laughed, a sound more like a *ribbet* than laughter. "Let's go, Barbie."

I looked at Quinn. "See you later. And thanks for the backup."

"No problem."

Carrow and I exited the pub, making our way out through the alley and back into Convent Garden. The toilet roll shop was closed, as usual, but the street itself had a few more people.

"Okay, pal," Mac said. "We're on your turf, and I've got no idea where to go."

"I've got this." Confidence suffused me. This *was* my turf. And I might not have been completely happy here, but I sure as hell knew my way around. "Come on. We'll catch the Tube."

"The Tube?"

"It's the Underground."

"Oh, right. The train that goes under the earth. You humans are crazy."

"You really don't come here much?"

"Why would I?" Mac asked. "You saw Guild City, it's great."

"Yeah, it was." I tugged on her. "Now come on."

We hurried to the nearest station, passing bustling bars and pubs and full flower boxes. Musicians played in front of the green and glass market building, and a wagon filled with flowers sat in the middle of the street as an art installation. It was one of my favorite parts of London, and I was glad that Mac got to see it when it was at its best.

We were nearly to the Underground station when I caught sight of a flyer in a pub window.

My face, staring straight out.

It was my College of Policing photo.

Oh, that burned.

Banks. That bastard. With the serial killer now in the news, he was under more pressure to catch someone, and he was trying to get me for it.

"You're on wanted posters?" Mac asked.

"Yeah." My stomach pitched. We had to fix this. *Now.*

I dragged Mac toward the sign over the stairs leading to the Underground. I reloaded my Oyster card to get us through the barriers, then found our platform, tapping my foot impatiently as I waited for the train to arrive.

When it did, we crammed in with everyone else. The ride itself was uneventful, besides the fact that Mac couldn't stop muttering, "Mind the gap," in different funny voices. Combined with her frog face, it was a real trip. One lady stared too long, and I explained that Mac was a makeup artist.

Mostly though, I kept my head tilted down to avoid the stares of men.

When the train reached our destination, I pulled Mac off and hurried up the stairs to the street.

"Thankfully, this part of town is quieter at night," I said.

"And more boring." Mac looked up at the towering buildings. The streets were nearly empty.

"That's good for us." I led us to the morgue, a building near the police station that I'd rarely visited. We found a good spot across the street from the entrance, and I pulled Mac into an alcove. Together, we stared at the two policemen who stood guard.

"Well, damn," Mac said. "How are we going to get in there?"

12

CARROW

Unfortunately, the cops on duty at the morgue looked alert and ready for anything.

"We really can't make a scene on the street," I said.

"Well, the entrance is inside an alcove." She pointed at the building. "And it looks like there are nooks on either side. If we could get them back in there, they'd be mostly hidden from the street."

"And do what, kill them?"

Mac's jaw dropped. "Uh, no."

"Whew. Because that is not my scene."

"No kidding. Otherwise, you wouldn't be trying to prove yourself innocent of a murder."

"True enough." I looked around warily, knowing that

all of London was out for my head. Corrigan's text messages made it clear enough, and now that I was in the real world again, I felt like I had a target on my back.

I shook the worries away and focused on the front door. "There's also a card scanner at the entrance. Everyone has a badge and has to swipe their way in."

"That's harder. There will be an alarm if we just break in, right?"

"Yeah. The police will have badges on them, though, I would think." At that moment, two people in long white lab coats exited the building, badges around their necks. "Ooh, look at them. They look official."

"Those coats would make us blend in if we ran into anyone in the hall."

"I like how you're thinking." The two figures nodded at the cops, then headed across the street toward the alley where we stood. "They're coming toward us. It's a sign."

"Let's follow them and borrow their stuff," Mac said.

"Borrow. Yeah. Borrow."

As they neared, I got a better look at their faces. The figure on the left was a slight man with pale hair and large glasses. The woman beside him was a bit taller, with a wild halo of dark curly hair and a stern expression. They reached our side of the street and turned left.

I peered after them, debating. "Are we just going to knock them out? They're scientists. They didn't exactly sign up for a life of random concussions."

"I've got it, don't worry. Come on." She left our alley and headed after them, walking quickly.

"What are you going to do?" I whispered.

"I'm a seer, but if I really put my power into it, I can disorient people with a touch." She shrugged. "Can't do it much, though. Takes a lot of power, then I have to recoup my strength."

"Let's try it, then."

She nodded.

Once we had turned a corner and were out of view of the policemen, we picked up the pace until we were only a meter behind the scientists. Their backs stiffened, and together, they looked back at us. I gave a huge smile, going for charmingly disarming, like someone who was looking for directions. Instead, they grimaced and cringed.

Okay, maybe I'd nailed creepy instead of disarming.

Mac's hands shot out, and she grabbed each person by the arm. Her magic pulsed briefly, and their eyes started to cross.

"It's working." Mac's voice sounded strained.

They stood there, swaying. I ran around behind them and tugged their white coats off. Mac made sure to keep contact with them as I yanked the white fabric from their shoulders. Last, I took the badges.

"I've got them," I said.

Mac let go, and they stared at her, dazed. Gently, she

pivoted them in the direction they'd been heading. She gave them a little nudge that set them walking.

I looked at her, brows raised. "Impressive."

"Yeah. I'm probably tapped out on that, though. Won't be able to play the same trick on the guards. Not unless we can wait a while for me to recoup my powers."

"Can't." I handed her a jacket and a badge. "Let's try our luck. Maybe they'll assume we're new and won't look at our credentials."

She nodded and shrugged into the jacket, then tugged the hood down from her face, since it just didn't go with the white coat.

"How do I look?" She gave a faint froggy cringe.

"Honestly, not that bad. You're still kind of green, but it's very faint now."

"Some of the magic from the hoodie is still working, just not as much as if I wore the hood."

"It'll have to do. You look like you ate bad seafood and maybe smooshed your nose on a door."

"Fantastic." She buttoned up the white coat.

I did the same, buttoning it so that it covered my jacket and hoodie. It was a lumpy combo, but it worked. I put the badge over my head next, and then Mac and I strode toward the morgue with confident strides that suggested we knew what we were doing.

We really didn't.

At least, I didn't.

I could wing it, though.

As we got close enough to see the guards' faces well, I gave a friendly nod. They did a double take at me and my new supermodel face, then frowned at Mac, who was slightly greener under the bright lights. Both men were of average height and build, with nondescript faces.

"Haven't seen you around," said the one on the left.

"New." I smiled, striding past him toward the door. "Have a good night."

"Good night." He nodded at me, smiling.

Victory!

"Hold on a moment," the one on the right said, his voice ringing with authority.

I nearly groaned. This was not what I needed right now. One out of two wasn't bad, except when it was two suspicious policemen. But it wasn't unexpected.

I gave a smile and turned to find him right behind me. The smiling guard had approached as well, and he stood in front of Mac, frowning at her.

Crap.

I eyed the alcove to my left. There were about two meters of space hidden behind a wall that faced the street. A bench sat there, out of the frequent rain and infrequent sun. There was an identical alcove on Mac's side of the entryway.

They were our best bets for doing this quietly.

I moved toward my alcove, and the policeman frowned at me. I hoped he'd follow so that I could try to knock him out with my limited self-defense skills, but he reached for his radio instead.

Damn it.

I lunged for him, grabbing his arm and yanking him toward me.

"What are you—"

I cut off his words with a quick, hard punch to the face. He stumbled backward, then surged toward me, shaking his head like a bull.

Crap. I so wasn't prepared for this.

I kicked out, nailing him in the stomach. He huffed out a breath and doubled over, then lunged upward and swung a punch for my head. I dodged, taking a glancing blow to the cheek that made my head ring.

To my left, Mac was landing a series of successful punches to her policeman. She either had a natural skill or spent Friday nights in a fight ring. Either way, I was impressed.

My skills, however, were sadly lacking. The guard lunged for me again, grabbing my arm in a tight grip. I kicked, my foot colliding with his thigh. He grunted but didn't let go.

Panic fluttered as I struck out, nailing him in the cheek again. He still didn't release me, and I began to feel like prey.

A flash of gray appeared from the corner of my eye, and a blur shot for the policeman's head. It collided with him, and a tiny blast of percussive magic slammed into him and echoed through the air, making my head pound.

The blur had been a raccoon—Cordelia?—and it dropped to the ground and ran away as the policeman began to fall.

Holy crap.

I grabbed the policeman at the last minute, stopping his unconscious body from slamming to the ground in a way that could give him a head injury. I wanted to get into the morgue, not kill the poor guy.

Assuming he was alive.

Oh please, be alive.

I leaned over him, feeling for his pulse.

There! Faint and reedy, but there.

My hand touched him, and a vision flashed in my mind. The policeman, driving his car later today. He crashed into another car.

Oh, crap.

I dug into his pocket, finding his keys and tossing them into the bushes where he'd never look. There. Problem solved. He couldn't drive his car, so he couldn't crash. I'd consider it a job well done.

I turned to see Mac leaning over her unconscious policeman, removing his handcuffs from his belt.

She looked up at me. "Cuff him. Tie his shoelaces together."

I did as she said, occasionally shooting worried glances at the policeman. "Will he be okay?"

"What happened to him? You knock him out?"

"No, that raccoon from Guild City showed up and bowled him over."

Mac looked up, her eyes wide. "A what from Guild City?"

"That raccoon I pointed out before. I swear it was Cordelia."

She pursed her lips. "Cordelia."

"Yeah. That was what I called her when I'd see her in the alley behind my old flat."

"Hmm."

"Hmm?" I groaned, tilting my head back. "That means you think I'm crazy, doesn't it?"

She shrugged. "Maybe. More likely, you're getting a familiar."

"Like, a witch's familiar?"

"Yeah, but you're not a witch. Not from your description of your powers." She looked around at the empty street, as if she'd just remembered where we were. "Actually, we should discuss this later."

"No kidding." I stood and dragged the policeman behind the bench. If someone looked closely, they'd find him, but it would have to do for now.

Mac did the same with her guy, and we met at the front door. I raised my badge and gave her a look. "We've got this."

"Totally."

"And thanks for your help."

She grinned. "I'm always up for an adventure."

"Well, I think this will deliver." I swiped the card, and the door buzzed. I pushed it open with my elbow, not wanting to leave any prints, and waited for Mac.

"I'd better scan this one. Just in case it counts how many people enter." She scanned, then followed me in.

Quickly, I pulled on a thin pair of leather gloves that I kept in my jacket pocket. I didn't want to leave any prints behind. Properly protected, I hurried to the wall, where a directory was posted. I searched it, finding my destination at the bottom. "Looks like it's in the basement."

"Ooh, perfectly creepy."

"Let's go." I strode toward the stairs, not wanting to get stuck in an elevator. The building echoed hollowly around us, and I doubted there were many more people here at this hour.

We took the stairs two at a time, reaching the morgue a minute later. I took mental stock of the potions that Eve had given me. They were shoved in my pockets, and I was grateful they hadn't broken in the scuffle with the guards.

The morgue was quiet and cold as we entered.

"He would have been a recent autopsy," I said, gazing at the wall covered in dozens of little metal doors where the bodies were kept on ice. Or whatever it was that they kept bodies on.

"Do you know his name?"

"No." I scanned the numbered doors. "Damn it, there are so many."

"Maybe the computer system will say. Or there might be notes on a desk."

We split up, searching the space. I didn't have much familiarity with the morgue, and the enormity of the task ahead of us was nerve-racking.

Then I heard the footsteps in the hall.

Oh, no.

I met Mac's gaze, and mouthed, "Hide."

13

Carrow

Mac and I flattened our backs against the wall on either side of the door. As the footsteps approached, I fingered the potions in my pocket, then withdrew the mind control one, carefully unscrewing the cap. When the figure entered, elation shot through me.

She wore a white coat like ours. A security guard might not know where my guy was, but this person would.

I dumped the powdery potion into my hand and jumped, grabbing the woman by her arm and yanking her toward me. She opened her mouth to scream, and I raised my hand, blowing the powder in her face.

She sucked in a lungful of the purple powder and went still.

"Holy crap, that worked," I said.

Mac grinned. "Of course. Eve is the best."

I looked at the woman, who had sleek red hair and blue glasses. Her green eyes were unfocused, but she was breathing normally.

"Tell me where the guy with the neck tattoo is located," I said. "He came in two nights ago with a bashed head."

She blinked, her face twisting in a grimace. Awareness flashed in her eyes, briefly, then anger and resistance. She could obviously feel the potion and fought it, but finally, her face crumpled in defeat. She turned and pointed to one of the little doors. "He's number thirteen."

"Lucky number thirteen," Mac said.

"Is he missing any organs?" I asked.

Her jaw clenched as she fought the potion that forced her to speak.

"Any missing organs?" I demanded.

"He's missing his—" Her eyelids fluttered, and she sagged, her eyes closing in exhaustion. I caught her, stopping her from slamming her head into the desk.

"That's all we'll get out of her," Mac said.

Gently, I laid her on the ground and strode to number thirteen. It was at waist level, and I reached for the handle.

It wasn't locked, and the door opened silently. I pulled the tray out, and the black bag containing the body was stark against the steel table.

I swallowed hard and looked up at Mac. "I don't suppose you have a fondness for dead bodies and want to do this bit?"

"What, look inside his chest?"

"No. Just open it and check who he is."

"Oh, well, in that case...no." She stepped back for good measure.

"Damn." I unzipped it, praying that there was only one guy with a neck tattoo and bashed-in head in the morgue.

It was my guy, at least according to the tattoo. I thought the head injury looked familiar, but they probably all looked similar when they were this gruesome. "It's him. Maybe we can check the records."

I unzipped the bag further, remembering that they often tied the identification to the toe. As expected, I found the little tag along with his official number and no name. I removed it and carried it over to the computer terminal.

Mac left her spot along the wall and joined me. "You know the password?"

"Nope." And the damned computer just sat silently, staring at me. Smug and locked. It took about two minutes to realize I had no chance of getting into the bloody thing. And there was no paperwork sitting out on the desk or other work surfaces.

Dread unfurled in my chest, and I looked at Mac. "None of Eve's potions figure out a computer password, will they?"

She grimaced and shook her head. "You're going to have to do it, aren't you?"

I nodded, my stomach pitching. "I don't even know what most of the organs look like."

Mac groaned. "Let's make it quick."

I nodded, turning back to the body. "This is the worst."

"Worse than going to prison?"

"Not worse than that." I moved on autopilot, my mind screaming in horror as I stared at the sewn-up Y-shaped incision on the man's chest.

Nope. There was no time to freak out, and even less time to wimp out.

I sucked in a breath, spun around, and found some tools on a side table. A pair of scissors beckoned, and I grabbed them, along with a clamp-like thing. I swapped out my leather gloves for some medical ones, working on autopilot.

I returned to the body and cut the stitches, then peeled the skin back.

"Oh, I'm going to faint." Mac sidled farther back.

I growled at Mac. "Don't brag. Not all of us have the luxury of passing out."

"I'll buy you a drink after this."

"A big one," I muttered, and considered the next gruesome task before me.

The inside of the man looked like a mess, but not in the way I'd anticipated. Instead of a jumble of organs, I found a handful of plastic bags stuffed in beneath the ribs like the world's goriest weekly shop. If I wanted to know what was missing, I'd have to open the bags and pray that I still remembered something from biology class.

"Damn it," I whispered, and removed the breastbone.

With my squeamish assistant standing well away from the corpse, I opened the bags and took my best guess at what I was seeing. The intestines were easy enough, as were the lungs and kidneys. Finally, by process of elimination, I realized what was missing.

"It's the heart," I said, willing my stomach not to give up the fight. If I puked on him, I would have to kill myself. I certainly couldn't continue living with that visual seared behind my eyes.

Hang on.

A weird burn mark distracted me from the disgusting thoughts. "What's this?"

"Don't make me look up close."

"Suck it up and get over here."

She groaned and joined me. We both stared into the chest cavity at the spot where the man's heart had once been. A symbol had been burned inside--three stars, overlapping.

"That was created by magic," Mac said.

"It has to be what the Devil sent me here to find." I frowned at it. "Is it the same as the necromancer's mark?"

"I don't think so. But why does he know so much about this murder?"

"That's what I want to know." I stripped off one of the gloves and yanked my mobile from my pocket, taking a picture. I got a few from different angles, but it was too dark.

I turned on the flash and took another picture.

A faint rumbling sounded, and I frowned. "Do you hear that?"

"Yeah, it's coming from—"

Black smoke billowed from the man's chest, rising straight from the symbol that had been burned into his flesh.

I jumped backward, but it was too late. The smoke wrapped around me, squeezing my limbs tight. "Mac!"

"I feel it, too." Her face was pinched tight with pain. "Hard to breathe."

I gasped, trying to get enough air into my lungs. Prickles raced over my skin like spiders. "What's happening?"

"Magic." She groaned, then said, "Curse them, Hecate. Oh, so mighty shall you be."

"What?"

"The witches." Her voice sounded even more squeezed.

Oh! The prank she'd played on them. The bust of Hecate that she'd poured a potion on should be screaming now. Thank fates, because this spell was making me start to feel weak.

"How will they find us?" It took all my strength to speak.

"If I don't respond, they'll use a locater charm."

"Respond?"

A voice sounded from the amulet around Mac's neck. "You clever bitch, Mac! Where are you? Stop this cursed thing right now!"

I could hear Hecate shrieking in the background like a horror movie victim. It was so loud that any nearby guards might hear.

I struggled against the magic that bound me, sucking more strength from me with every second. My vision was starting to blur and my legs to tremble.

"I can't answer them," Mac said. "Not without touching the charm."

Shit, shit, shit.

I tried to hobble to her, hoping I could press my forehead against the charm. Or maybe fall against her.

Instead, I toppled over onto the ground, hitting it so hard that my vision went black for a moment. Footsteps sounded from the floor above. Or maybe that was my imagination.

Were guards coming?

Was I going to be discovered here, next to the torn-open body of the victim?

Fear chilled my skin.

"My, my, what have we here?" A feminine voice sounded from my left.

Out of the corner of my eye, I barely caught sight of Coraline. She stood in a cloud of pink light, somehow projecting her form into the morgue. Her dark hair was streaked with green that matched the brilliant emerald of her eyes. She tapped her foot, staring at us. "Got yourself into quite a pickle, Mac."

"Get us out of here, and I'll tell you the code to shut her up."

"Oh, you will, all right." Coraline raised her hands and began to chant. Magic sparked around her palms, and a faint white light surrounded Mac and me.

The evil that gripped us so tightly seemed to loosen, but Coraline didn't stop chanting. Her brow furrowed from the effort, and she grimaced. "Powerful dark magic."

Her own power continued to work, and I struggled, finally able to move my limbs a bit. Coraline grunted and forced more of her magic toward us.

"Hurry," Mac said. "Guards are coming. Humans."

"You idiots." Coraline shoved another blast of magic

at us, and the darkness that bound me finally disappeared.

I gasped, scrambling to my feet.

"The code, Mac," Coraline demanded.

"Macbeth O'Connell is the most amazing Magica ever," Mac said.

"Seriously?" Coraline raised her brows.

"Say that, and Hecate will shut up." Mac grinned. "Can we get a ride back to Guild City with your nice portal there?"

"No." Coraline and her pink light disappeared.

"Damn it." Mac turned to me. "We need to get a move on."

"No kidding."

I turned back to the body as a pair of guards burst into the room. Both were men of average height but grim demeanors, though their faces blanched when they saw the results of my amateur autopsy spread out around the room.

"Raise your hands," demanded the younger one, who couldn't have been more than twenty-five.

Instead, I shoved my hand into my pocket and drew out a freezing charm. I chucked the thing at them, praying it would work. The dusty blue cloud exploded into the air, and the men froze solid.

"That ought to buy us a few minutes." I turned back to the body. There was no point in trying to put it back together. The guards had seen what we were doing. Fortunately, I still didn't look like me.

I grabbed a plastic bag and shoved my gross gloves in them, then put it in my pocket, not wanting to leave anything with my fingerprints behind. I put my leather gloves on, then wiped the scissors and clamp off with a paper towel, getting rid of any prints, and returned them to the table.

Mac and I hurried from the room, skirting around the frozen guards and moving as quickly as we could without full-on running. We made it to the top floor and strode toward the main exit.

I prayed there were no other guards in the building.

We were nearly to the main doors when they opened, and two new cops walked in.

Shit.

They both got a good look at our faces, and I prayed the potions were still working.

"Other way," I whispered, and we spun on our heels and hightailed it deeper into the building.

"Hey, you there!" shouted one of the cops.

"Run." I sprinted down the hall, fumbling in my pocket for the other freezing potion bomb.

Finally, my fingers closed around it. I grabbed it and chucked it behind me, looking back in time to see it explode in front of one of the cops. He froze solid, but the other one wasn't in the line of fire. He kept running for us, face twisted in a grimace.

I sprinted on, pushing myself until my lungs burned. Mac easily kept up, as her legs were longer than mine. We raced down the hall, taking the first right, and sprinted to the end. An office on our right had an open door, and we dashed inside. A large window beckoned, showing the street beyond.

"Thank fates we're on street level." Mac grabbed the chair from behind the desk and tossed it at the window. The glass shattered.

Wow, breaking out of windows was getting to be a habit with me.

An alarm shrieked as we climbed out and landed on the pavement. We sprinted away from the building. I looked back in time to see the officer lean out the window, his gaze on mine.

Oh, please don't catch us.

14

Carrow

Mac and I raced away from the morgue. Behind us, the cop jumped out of the window, tripped, and landed on his knees.

Oh, thank God for luck.

We ran faster, leaving him behind as we turned one street corner, and then another. As we sprinted down the pavement, we tore off our stolen white coats, chucking them into an alley as we passed. I kept the badge since that probably had my fingerprints on it. Police sirens sounded from a street away, and my heartbeat thundered.

"Are those for us?" Mac demanded.

"Oh, yeah, they're for us."

"Damn it. I don't want to go to human jail."

"Same." We turned right, and I spotted a cab. With the cops on our tail and the Tube station still several streets away, it was worth the splurge. I shot my hand up in the air, praying.

The cab spotted us, changing lanes to come to a stop at the curb.

"Thank you." I climbed in, Mac following. "Covent Garden," I told the driver. "The market."

If the cops made the connection between us and this cabbie—unlikely, but I was paranoid—I didn't want to lead them straight to the Haunted Hound.

He nodded. "Be there in a jiff."

My heart thundered the whole way to Convent Garden, then the entire way to the Haunted Hound. Once we made it to the safety of the pub, Mac sagged against the door. "Thank fates we're back."

"They can't get in here?" I asked, searching the small crowd warily. No one turned toward us but Quinn, who smiled at us from the bar.

"Not unless they have magic." Mac straightened. "Now, it's time for a drink."

"And they don't. Have magic, I mean." Finally, I relaxed.

Mac looked at me, her eyes wide. "You changed back."

"To myself?"

"Yeah."

"So did you. When did that happen?"

"I don't know. I was in such a panic, I wouldn't have noticed."

"Could it have been when the guards were chasing us?"

"Maybe."

Shit. They had looked right at us. Had they seen my real face after all?

I drew in a shuddering breath. They might not get me for the murder, but I didn't want to be caught desecrating a body. I rubbed my hands over my face.

Mac grabbed my arm. "Come on. Let's get that drink. I'd say we earned it."

"Yeah. Yeah."

She pulled me toward the bar, where Quinn waited. Handsome as ever, he eyed us up and down, taking in our disheveled appearances and heavy breathing. "Have fun, ladies?"

"Sure." I sat, staring at the offerings behind the bar, having no idea what I wanted. My mind spun with everything that had happened.

"Two Hound's Prides," Mac said.

"Coming right up."

"What's a Hound's Pride?" I asked.

"Does it matter?"

"Not really, actually."

"That's what I thought." She grinned. "But it's just a local ale, made here."

"Great. Perfect."

Quinn set two pints in front of us, and I grabbed one gratefully, drinking half of it in huge gulps. I looked up at Mac. "What the hell was the dark magic that froze us like that?"

"Necromancer magic, probably."

"Did my mobile's flash make it go off?"

Mac shrugged. "Maybe it didn't like the light. And you did reveal his work."

"But...why? What was the point?"

"There probably was no point. It could be a magical remnant of the spell that was performed when the person was murdered. All magic decays, and when it does, dangerous things can happen."

"How is it different than the little spiral shaped burn mark?" I asked.

"The spiral is the generic mark of the necromancer. That big star burn is something else entirely. Part of his magic, yes, but it's more specific." Mac shrugged. "I don't know exactly what it means."

Eve appeared at my side as I set the pint down. She wore a flowing purple dress, and her wings glittered under the lights over the bar. Her raven flew behind her, but no one acknowledged the bird, so I didn't either. That topic seemed to be off-limits. She took a seat next to me. "You finished with your mission?"

"Yes. Thank you for the potions. They saved our butts."

"Success?"

Mac grinned. "Yeah, I'd say so."

Mac, Eve, and Quinn all stared at me, radiating helpful energy.

"Well, what'd you find?" Eve asked.

I pulled the mobile out of my pocket. Normally, I wouldn't share my clues with anyone. Now, I had a lovely, weird magical crew that seemed willing to help me, and it was freaking cool.

I pulled up the picture and laid the mobile on the bar.

Everyone leaned over to look at it.

"Ew," Eve said. The raven sitting behind her on the table twitched.

I grimaced in sympathy. "Truer words never spoken."

"I don't recognize that symbol," said Quinn.

"Neither do I," Eve replied. "But the necromancer took the heart."

"What kind of spell could he or she perform with it?" I asked.

"I don't know," Mac said. "All sorts, I guess. Maybe he's trying to create more power with it."

I looked at Eve and Quinn, who both shrugged. I couldn't help but wonder what Beatrix's body had been used for, but I forced the thought back. Dwelling on it would only distract me, and in a bad way. But since my friends had no more information…

I slugged back the last of my ale and put the mobile away. "Right. I think I need a word with the Devil."

~

Mac had agreed to let me see the Devil alone. She'd wanted to come as backup, but it was too dangerous. He couldn't control my mind, which made me the perfect person to interrogate him about the symbol inside the body.

He'd expected it to be there, or at least, he'd expected *something* to be there.

I needed to know why.

Eve had given me a small assortment of protective potions—on the house, she'd said. I still planned to pay her back someday, somehow.

As I strode toward the Devil's tower, I felt a presence alongside me. I looked left and right, finally spotting Cordelia running along the other side of the street, keeping pace with me. The fat little raccoon was fast.

"What are you doing, Cordelia?" I called, feeling crazy for talking to her like this. It was one thing to chat with her while I was drinking my boxed wine and knowing she'd never respond.

But this?

I almost expected her to say something back to me.

Cordelia, however, didn't so much as glance at me.

And as we neared the vampire's tower, she turned left down an alley and disappeared.

Weird.

When I reached the edge of the clearing in front of the vampire's tower, I stopped and stared at it.

He probably wasn't the murderer, right?

Right.

I swallowed hard and stepped forward. He was certainly dangerous, and he very well might know a lot about the murderer, but my gut said he wasn't the killer. It also said that he knew something valuable about the crime.

Just in case, though, I stuck my hand into the pocket of my leather jacket and let my fingertips brush across the smooth glass surfaces of the potion bombs that Eve had given me. Freezing, healing, and smoke.

I had backup. And Mac had sworn to come get me if I didn't contact her in an hour. It was more than I'd ever had before, and I was grateful.

As I neared the two guards, I recognized them. Once again, they made me think of animals—lions and panthers. Just like Quinn. Their massive hands were folded in front of their bodies as they stared impassively at me.

I opened my mouth to request an audience with their boss, but the one on the left just turned and opened the door for me, gesturing for me to enter.

Quickly, I glanced between the two of them, not sure if I liked this kind of welcome.

Not that it necessarily mattered. I had to go in, whether I liked it or not. I gave the city behind me one last look, then strode through the doors. The hostess who waited for me was the same, and she inclined her head. "Welcome back."

"Expecting me?"

She smiled and shrugged. "Come this way."

She led me through the club again. Tonight, it was heaving. The hour was just past midnight, and the chairs and tables were full. A band played onstage—a trio of women with snakes for hair. Everyone in the place avoided looking right at them, though they were dancing along to the music.

Would the patrons turn to stone if they met the gazes of the three gorgons?

Between that and the lava room at the witches' party, it was clear these supernaturals liked some danger with their nights out.

The halls we walked down were as confusing as ever, and I could feel my mind starting to fuzz. Whatever had been in the air last time was here again, making it difficult to determine where I was in the building. If I returned, I'd never find my way back without a guide.

The hostess stopped at the wooden door and knocked. I heard nothing, but she must have picked up a signal, because after a pause, she let us in.

I followed her into the room, realizing that the Devil was alone this time. The two guards no longer stood behind his desk, and I wondered if he had dismissed them right before I arrived.

"A guest for you, sir," the hostess said.

"I can see that, Miranda. Thank you." He didn't so much as look at her. No—the entire time, his gaze was glued to me.

Miranda slipped out the door, shutting it noiselessly behind her.

Silence hung heavy in the air as I inspected him. He was as impossibly handsome as I remembered, lounging in the chair behind his desk. His broad shoulders filled out his suit perfectly, and his gray tie lay flat against his muscular chest. I could imagine him strangling someone with that tie, and I wasn't sure what that said about me.

I shook the thought away.

"Please sit." He gestured to the chair in front of his desk.

I looked at it like it was a snake. If I sat, it would be that much harder to fight back. To run. "No, thank you."

"Understood." He stood, his movements graceful, and walked around the side of the desk.

I stepped back, determined to keep my distance. The memory of his touch sent heat shivering through me, and I didn't need that kind of distraction. I had no idea why I was kind of into the fear—probably some predator magic of his making me feel this way—but I certainly didn't need to encourage it.

"Well?" he asked. "Did you find your man?"

"First, I need to clear something up."

"Yes?"

"When you are looking for me, *don't* use your mind control powers on my friends."

"What do you mean?"

"You used mind control on my friend Eve. Don't do that. Ever."

"Friends already, are you?"

"Yeah, and I don't have many of those, so I'm going to protect her."

A small smile tugged at his lips. "I quite like you."

"It's not mutual. And it never will be if you treat my friends like that." I couldn't imagine ever *liking* him. It was such a weak word for a man like him. Loathe, lust, love.

Love?

Where had that one come from?

Insane to even think the word. It had to be magic. Hell, in this world, anything I didn't like I could explain away with magic. Convenient.

I gave him a hard look. "Before we go any further, I need to know why you are interested in this murder."

"Murder is always interesting."

"Don't try to smooth-talk me. I'm still not one

hundred percent convinced you don't have some role to play in this."

"Yet you returned here?" Concern flickered across his face. "You should protect yourself better. If you think I'm involved, you shouldn't be here. It's dangerous, and I don't like it."

"You know nothing about me."

"I'd like to change that. For example, you seem *very* invested in this murder."

"Um, I'm wanted for a string of serial killings. My face is on posters in pubs. Of course I'm invested in clearing my name." My throat tightened at the thought of Beatrix.

"That's not the only reason."

"How do you know?"

He shrugged. "I don't know. I can feel it."

"Some bastard killed my friend, okay?" The words burst out of me. "My only friend, a year ago. And I found her dead."

"The woman you asked me about." His voice was softer.

"Yes. And there were no leads until this guy ended up dead with the same little spiral burn on his neck."

He nodded. "I see. I'm sorry."

I shook away the thoughts, hardening my face as I crossed my arms over my chest and raised an eyebrow. "Tell me more about *your* interest in this murder."

I could tell from his dissatisfied expression that he

wanted to ask me more about Beatrix, but he just nodded. "Fine. I like to keep track of everything that happens in this city. And I believe that there may be a necromancer in town."

Just like Mac suspected. "And that's bad?"

"Exceedingly. They are powerful, dangerous, and unscrupulous. There is one particular necromancer that I've clashed with since I came to England."

"From where?"

"I thought you didn't want to get to know each other."

"Fine." I didn't really need that information, anyway. "So you think the killer might be this necromancer?"

"Yes. And I think he might be up to something that threatens me and my empire. An acquaintance tipped me off that he came into town about a year ago. At the same time, a valuable dagger of mine was stolen. Perhaps by him."

"You think he used it in the murder."

"It was capable of great magic, so yes, it is possible. When our victim was killed, there was a flare of magic—likely from a spell performed at the time. I tracked that magic and was going to investigate the scene when you showed up."

I supposed the story worked. And the flare of magic described the crazy symbol inside the victim's chest. There was no way I'd be letting my guard down, though. "You have no idea what this necromancer is after?"

"No."

"Why haven't you looked for him, then? Why give me clues?"

"Because you're competent and skilled and will get the job done. Leaving me free to spend my time on other things."

"Like?" He'd better be trying to solve this damned murder, too, if I was going to trust him.

"I've been hunting the necromancer here in Guild City."

"Caught him yet?"

"Sadly, no." His voice had a wry lilt that I liked. "But there have been flares of dark magic at the churches surrounding Guild City. Ones in the human realm."

"That's strange that he would be in the human realm."

"Not that strange. Many supernaturals live and work there. You've just never seen them."

"Right. Say I believe you. Say you have nothing to do with this at all. Where do we go from here? Do you have any clues for me?"

"I was rather hoping you'd have some for me."

"I did find something." I hesitated.

He moved nearer, his steps slow, as if he wanted to avoid startling me. I thrust out a hand. "No closer."

"Nervous?"

His mind control power didn't work on me, but that didn't mean I wasn't afraid of him. "You're a vampire, for God's sake. With fangs and maybe even super speed."

"Yes to both, but I don't attack unarmed women."

"Armed ones?"

"Rarely. And only if they're out for my head."

"I suppose that's fair."

He shrugged. "I'm a feminist vampire."

"Vlad the Impaler is a feminist?"

"Searching for history?"

"I don't even know your name. Everyone just calls you the Devil."

"If it fits...."

"It does. But I'd like a name."

"Grey."

"As in shadows?"

"As in Gardens."

My jaw nearly dropped at the joke. He could joke? "Grey Gardens?"

"Of *course* as in shadows." He leaned against the desk. "Now, do you trust me enough to tell me what you found in the body?"

I dug my mobile out of my pocket and pulled up the picture so that he could see it. Maybe he would know more than Mac had. "His heart was missing. And this symbol was burned inside."

A small smile stretched across his face, a smile of pure satisfaction.

"You know what it is?" I demanded.

"Not exactly. But I know we can use it to track the killer."

"Couldn't we have used the spiral-shaped burn mark to track him?"

"No. That's a generic mark of necromancer magic. Small and untrackable because it contains so little magic." He pointed to the phone. "*That* is evidence of powerful magic. Big enough to leave a stain on the victim and the murderer. The Sorcerers' Guild can perform a spell that will locate the person who also bears this mark on their soul. That will be our killer."

"Holy crap, we're close?"

"Perhaps. Would you like to come with me?"

"To the Sorcerers' Guild?"

"Yes." He nodded. "For a price, they'll track our killer."

"You're paying?"

"Of course."

"Okay, let's do it."

He nodded, another satisfied smile stretching across his handsome face. Somehow, I felt trapped, the first course of this vampire's dinner.

15

The Devil

Satisfaction roared through me when Carrow agreed to visit the Sorcerers' Guild at my side. I'd told her the truth about the necromancer and his likely goals—but I didn't like hearing that the entire police force was after her. It roused a protective instinct in me I'd thought long dead. Guild City was a fine place to live, but being unable to return to London would make it a cage.

"Come." I strode around her, inhaling her scent as I passed.

Lavender.

And something intrinsically *her* that I liked very much but couldn't identify. Both scents were so faint that I drew in the aroma more deeply just to get the barest taste of it. Oh, how I wished I could smell her better. It made me feel more alive, somehow. Reminding me that I'd only been existing these many years—not truly living.

Ice man.

The strongest urge surged through me to turn around and pull her into my arms. I resisted, moving toward the door without looking back at her. She found my intense attention uncomfortable, and I needed to remember that. For now.

Not to mention, every second I spent with her, I wanted to bite her. I hadn't wanted to bite someone in centuries.

But her…

Yes.

I shook away the thought as best I could and strode down the hall.

Her footsteps caught up to mine, and she joined me, shoulder to shoulder.

"You have a contact at the Sorcerers' Guild?" she asked.

"I have contacts everywhere."

"What now? Do we walk up and knock on their door?"

"Not quite. But we will walk there."

"Yeah. No cars in town, right?"

"Just motorcycles."

"You don't ride?"

"Who needs a ride when I can turn into a bat and fly?"

She choked. "You...what?"

"Joking."

"I didn't think vampires had a sense of humor."

I shrugged. "We are enigmas."

She huffed a dry laugh.

The club was busy as we passed through, but the crowd parted before us. It was a perk of owning the place. Of owning the whole town, actually. People got out of my way.

We passed the hostess stand, and I leaned closer to Miranda.

"Yes, sir?"

"If I'm not back by closing, see that the shifters come to the Sorcerers' Guild. They're to find Carrow and get her out."

She nodded. "Consider it done."

"Thank you."

The night air welcomed Carrow and me, the moon shining bright over the city in front of us.

"What was that about shifters?" Carrow asked.

"The shifters are my bodyguards, though I don't bring them with me often. And the Sorcerers' Guild doesn't . . . like me. If it doesn't go well there today, the shifters will rescue you."

"What about you?"

"I'll be dead."

She stumbled, and I stopped to meet her gaze. I raised an eyebrow. "Yes?"

"You'll be…dead?"

"It's highly unlikely. But if we do run into trouble, I'll get you out of there or die trying."

Her jaw slackened a bit. And frankly, the words shocked me as well. This urge to protect…I'd never felt it before, but it was real. It hung from me like an ill-fitting coat, but one that felt somehow natural.

"If you think you're going to die, why not bring the shifters with us?"

"As I said, highly unlikely. Paranoia is suffocating. But being prepared is the only way to make it in this world."

"True enough." She started walking again, and I joined her. "Where is this place?"

"Two towers over. Not far."

We walked in silence, but I found myself itching to ask about her. What was her life like on the outside? Who was she?

This strange curiosity was unsettling.

Fortunately, there was more than enough to distract me on the streets of Guild City. The streets between my tower and that of the Sorcerers' Guild were a party zone, and the bars were busy. We passed drunken supernaturals of all kinds, and I could feel her interest.

"Have you not met many supernaturals before?" I asked, unable to help myself.

"No. Not until the murder."

"What do you mean?"

"I didn't know this world existed."

"But you're part of it."

"On the outskirts, at best." She sounded wistful, and I wanted to fix whatever made her feel left out.

What the hell was *happening* to me?

"How is that possible?" I asked.

"None of your business."

Maybe, but I wanted to know more about her. I wanted to know everything about her. I craved the information like I'd once craved blood. Like I craved her blood.

I was going insane.

Fortunately, we'd arrived at the Sorcerers' Guild. It provided a welcome distraction.

The tower was taller than any other guild tower, a monstrosity of dark gray granite that speared the night sky and dwarfed the towers around it. Only the clock tower was larger, and it was on the other side of town.

"Creepy." Carrow started toward the front door, an enormous black thing studded with iron.

I reached for her, then clenched my hand into a fist, drawing it back. I couldn't touch her. If I did, I might not stop.

"Not that way." My voice was rusty.

She turned, brows raised. "That's the door."

"Precisely. We can't enter that way. Come." I turned

and walked toward the city wall to the left of the tower, heading for a set of stairs secreted in the stone. I pressed my hand against a rough surface, and a section of the wall slid away, revealing the hidden steps.

I ascended quickly, and she followed. Despite her light footsteps, it was impossible not to be aware of her.

The top of the wall was empty at this hour, and I turned left toward the tower soaring upward. The stone was dark and smooth, rising high into the sky.

"So, this place is full of sorcerers?" Carrow asked.

"Yes. They specialize in spells."

"Don't the witches do that?"

"Yes, but different types of spells. The witches will sell you spells to take on your way. Useful things, but often not quite as powerful or dangerous as what the sorcerers sell." I slanted her a look. "That's not to say the witches aren't as powerful as the sorcerers. They're more so, but they don't share their strongest magic."

"Untrusting?"

"Very. Each guild has a motto. Theirs is, 'We are the daughters of the witches you could not burn.'"

"They got caught up in the witch burnings?"

I nodded. "And they haven't forgotten."

"So then, if you want something powerful, you come to the sorcerers, and they sell it to you?"

"Exactly. But they insist on performing the spell, too. Unlike the witches, they don't sell spells to go."

"No magical takeaway from these guys, huh?"

I felt a smile crack my face and forced it back. "No."

"What's their motto?"

"'Our own, first. Always.'"

"It sounds like they wouldn't spit on you if you were on fire."

"That's accurate." I stopped in front of the stone wall. There was nothing here—no door or window or light fixture. At least, not that the eye could see. Quickly, I located the stone that I wanted and tapped twice.

Pale magic sparked in the air, and faint wisps of light swirled in front of the stone.

"What are you doing?" Carrow asked.

"Secret entrance. Most of the sorcerers . . . don't like me."

"But you *do* have a contact inside?"

"I do, and this door was built especially for my use."

"This is who you are, then? Someone who has secret power all over the city, lurking around like a giant bat?"

A rare grin cracked my face, and I almost felt a laugh rise to the surface. Almost. I looked down at her. "A giant bat?"

"You're the one who made the flying joke." She grinned up at me, so beautiful in the moonlight that it hurt to look at her. The glow of the moon seemed to give her a bit of extra color that my turned eyes couldn't normally pick up.

My gaze lingered on the smooth skin of her throat, and I swallowed hard. There was something about her

—about her energy and her spirit, as strange as it sounded—that called to me. I couldn't compel her, and I liked that. But it was more than that. It was strange to feel so much so quickly...and bloody uncomfortable.

"You know, because you're a vampire," she clarified.

I'd been staring at her in silence for too long, and she'd taken it for confusion. "I understand," I said.

"Are you really hundreds of years old?" She searched my face, avoiding my eyes. "Really Vlad the Impaler?"

Guilt streaked through me, so visceral and real that I almost twitched. Those memories were long buried—for my own sanity. I'd done things I wasn't proud of, and in terrible moments, I wondered if I'd wanted to do them.

I had.

It had been more than the blood lust and insanity of a newly turned vampire.

I'd wanted to do terrible things.

The wall in front of me began to dissolve, and I turned to it, grateful for the interruption. I could feel her gaze on me as the wall disappeared entirely.

A pale man stood there, tall and broad-shouldered and wearing the long black cloak of the Sorcerers' Guild. I felt a streak of annoyance as Carrow's attention shifted to Remington. I didn't want her to look at him. I wanted her gaze on me, always.

"Devil." Remington nodded his head, his eyes going to Carrow. He frowned. "And a guest?"

"Indeed."

"This is unusual."

"Don't think too deeply about it." I had no intention of introducing Carrow. She was mine, though she didn't know it yet, and Remington was powerful and dangerous. I didn't want him to get too interested in her.

"I'm Carrow Burton," she said.

I stifled an annoyed noise. I should have anticipated that Carrow would do whatever the hell she wanted. I hadn't known her long, but I did know that.

"Remington, Sorcerers' Guild."

"I can see that." Her gaze moved over the building. "Nice place you have here."

Remington's brows rose. *Nice place.*

I nearly chuckled again. That was two times she'd nearly made me laugh, two times in hundreds of years. It made my throat feel strange, and I resisted rubbing it.

"Come." Remington turned and led us into a darkened stairwell, a magical and secret set of stairs that he'd created.

We strode up the dark, narrow steps, six stories that rose up and up, until we arrived at the roof. Remington opened the hatch at the top of the tower, and we followed him out and into the open air.

It always felt closer to the moon up here, something that I enjoyed. One of the few things I enjoyed these days. A faint breeze blew across the top of the tower, bringing the scent of rain with it. The city sprawled beneath us, ancient streets twisting alongside each other, golden streetlamps glowing.

Remington turned to us. "What can I do for you, Devil?"

I held out my hand to Carrow. "Your mobile, please."

She pulled it out of her pocket and fiddled with it for a moment. When she handed it to me, the image of the body was on the screen. The burn mark was clear—two stars overlapping each other. I showed it to Remington. "We want to track whoever made this mark."

He studied it a moment, a frown stretching across his face. "A necromancer?"

"We believe so."

He grimaced. "Best find him soon, then."

"My thoughts exactly."

"Give me a moment, and I'll get what I need." Remington strode back to the stairs.

"He won't be long." I handed Carrow her mobile back.

"He'll do the spell up here?"

"It seems so."

She looked like some kind of ancient goddess with the wind blowing her hair back from her face and intensity gleaming in her eyes. "Why didn't you answer my question down on the wall?"

Bloody hell. She wasn't going to let that one go. "Are you happy in the human world?"

She frowned. "You're changing the subject."

"You're quick."

"And not susceptible to flattery."

"Answer my question, and perhaps I'll answer yours."

"I don't like the sound of that *perhaps*."

"It's the best you'll get."

"Fine." She crossed her arms over her chest. "I am happy in the human world."

"No, you're not."

"You don't know me."

"I'd like to."

She hesitated at that, surprise flashing across her face. "Really?"

"Very much." My candor startled me. I rarely shared my thoughts with anyone. Unnecessary when I could get whatever I wanted. I was *very* good at getting my own way. "Tell me. Are you happy in the real world? The human one?"

"What is happy?"

"That's a no, then."

She shrugged. "It's my home."

"It doesn't have to be."

She looked past me, out at the city. Her face turned wistful, and something tightened in my heart. I grimaced, barely resisting rubbing my chest.

Feelings.

I didn't like them.

Unfortunately, around her, it seemed impossible not to have them.

"What is it about the human world that you like?"

She blinked at me, seeming confused. "My books from Beatrix, I suppose. Cordelia."

"Who is Cordelia?"

"A raccoon."

"What?"

"I like her, okay? She lives in the alley behind my flat. Or at least, I thought she did."

I couldn't do anything about a raccoon. But the books... "Your books? Surely you could bring those here."

"Maybe."

"Maybe? That doesn't make any sense. They are just books. They can be taken from London to Guild City."

"I'd need to go back and get them, and as it stands, I'm a wanted woman." A shadow crossed her face. "There's every chance the police have taken them into evidence."

"Well, with any luck, we'll have you off the hook for that crime soon. And we'll avenge your friend."

"It may be too late."

"It's never too late." That was a bloody lie. It was often too late. I'd learned that the hard way. "But if that's all you have there, I see no reason why you would stay in the human world."

She was silent for a moment, and I could see the

thoughts turning behind her eyes. "What about you? I answered you. Your turn."

My enhanced hearing picked up the sound of footsteps, and I grinned. "I believe Remington is returning."

"You haven't answered my questions."

"Alas, I have not."

"That's not fair."

"It certainly isn't."

∼

Carrow

I grumbled, giving the Devil one last annoyed look. He'd told me his name was Grey, but it was still hard to think of him that way.

Remington appeared through the trap door, a leather bag in his hands. He approached, asking, "Could I see that image again?"

I pulled out my mobile, showing the picture to Remington. He studied it for a moment, then nodded. "That's all I need, thank you."

Quickly, I put the mobile back in my pocket. The Devil stood next to me. His face was impassive as the sorcerer reached inside his leather bag. This was old hat to him, but magic still astounded me.

He still astounded me.

A vampire, and one who so quickly saw to the heart of me. Who distracted me so easily. Who played me like a fiddle.

I didn't like it.

I stepped away from him, determined to ignore him. It wasn't easy when his scent wrapped around me, rich and delicious. I wanted to breathe him in. Hell, I just wanted to stand in his presence and feel whatever strange connection it was that we had. I was afraid of him, I didn't particularly like him, but damn if he didn't make me feel good just by standing next to me.

Alive. That's how I felt. So alive that I vibrated with it.

In the human world, I'd existed, a shadow life in a shadow world. There, but not there. Half dead, even. Just me and Cordelia and my little single-size boxes of wine.

And now I was here, and the world seemed so big and open and amazing.

Remington pulled various vials of potion out of his bag and poured them on the ground like paint, drawing a pattern that matched the image on my phone. The symbol that had been carved—or burned—into the victim's chest appeared on the rooftop, two meters wide, a perfect duplicate at a larger scale.

As Remington finished, the moon began to glow more brightly. A ray of light shone from it, strong and distinct, illuminating the symbol on the rooftop.

"What's happening?" I asked.

"The moonlight will find your murderer," he explained. "It helps that it's nearly the full moon—the spell will be stronger. It is searching Guild City and then London, looking for whoever created the symbol in the body of your victim."

Wow. "How long will it take?"

Remington gave a faint shrug. "It depends on where your murderer is. Could be minutes or hours."

"Could you alert me when it is done?" the Devil asked.

"I will, yes."

"Thank you, Remington." The Devil reached into his pocket, withdrew something small I couldn't see, and passed it to Remington. The sorcerer took it and appeared satisfied. That done, the Devil turned to me. "Shall we go?"

"Is that it?"

"Unless you want to stay up here, it is."

"All right, let's go."

I gave Remington a last nod of thanks, then followed the Devil off the roof. We made our way back to the city wall in silence. When we reached it, the Devil said, "I'll walk you back to where you are staying."

"You don't have to do that."

"Do you know your way?"

"I do." We'd taken a circuitous route to get there—all of the routes seemed that way in this ancient city—but I thought I could find my way back to Mac's place. "I have a good sense of direction."

"I'll walk you anyway." He strode toward the stairs that led down from the wall.

I hurried after him, knowing there was no point in arguing.

As we walked, I tried to ask him about the Vlad the Impaler stuff, but he didn't answer. Irritating, but I didn't press it. He was still a vampire, after all. And even though he hadn't bitten me, he'd definitely been looking at my neck more than I liked.

He stopped at the green door that led to Mac's stairs and turned to me. "I'll let you know when I know something."

"Thank you."

He didn't wait for me to say anymore, and I wasn't sure if I was going to. There were questions I still wanted to ask, but I hadn't come up with the guts.

As the Devil disappeared down the street, I knocked on the door. A few seconds later, her voice sounded from above me. I looked up, spotting her hanging out of the window and grinning. "Hey there! Any luck?" she called.

"Yeah."

"Come on up. It's open."

I pushed my way inside, climbing the stairs to her flat. The door was open to the stairwell, and Quinn and

Eve were inside, drinking a beer. The raven sat on the windowsill. It was well after midnight.

"The Haunted Hound closed, so we were having a little after-party," Mac said. "And waiting for you."

"Worried?" I asked.

"With the Devil as your companion?" Eve raised an eyebrow. "Yes."

"Are you really not susceptible to his mind control?" Quinn asked.

"I'm not."

Eve hummed. "That's interesting."

"I'm really the only one?" I couldn't believe it.

"Really and truly," Mac said.

I whistled low under my breath.

"Where are you with the murderer?" Mac asked.

I told them about the Sorcerers' Guild and Remington and the finding spell, not leaving anything out. He hadn't told me that any of it was meant to be a secret, and I considered Mac my ally here. Quinn and Eve, too.

"He's got his own secret entrance to the Sorcerers' Guild?" Eve's brows rose.

"Yep. And Remington at his beck and call."

"Can't say I'm surprised," Quinn said. "His power goes deeper than any of us know."

"Was he mind-controlling Remington?" Mac asked.

"Not that I could tell."

"You'd be able to tell," Eve said. "Remington's eyes

would have gone slightly unfocused, and he'd have seemed a bit off."

"That didn't happen," I said.

"Now that I know you're safe, I'm getting out of here," Quinn said.

"Do you live nearby?" I asked.

"Top floor of the building next door. Right next to the empty unit above Mac."

"I'm right beneath him," Eve said. "And believe me, he sounds like a freaking buffalo when he's walking around."

Envy wasn't my favorite emotion, but I was feeling it in spades. What would it be like to live close to people I liked instead of the weirdos at my flat block in London? Cordelia was great, but she was a raccoon. It was time for some real friends again.

The Devil's questions echoed in my mind. Why didn't I live here? Why shouldn't I?

16

The Devil

I couldn't sleep, but that wasn't unusual. Sleep wasn't a companion of mine. But normally, I would find respite for at least a few hours each night.

Not tonight.

The clock said that it had only been an hour since I'd seen her.

It felt like more.

I raked a hand through my hair, disgusted. I was behaving like a besotted idiot.

A knock sounded at the door of my office, followed by Miranda's soft voice. "The Oracle, here to see you, sir."

"Send her in."

The door creaked, and the Oracle drifted through it before it was fully open, her form partially transparent. As she stopped in front of my desk, she turned fully corporeal, her face flickering from old to young. She had a strange magic that even I didn't understand, but I liked that she was nearly as old as I was. Made me feel less alone, though we rarely saw each other.

"Thank you for not just barging in." My tone was wry. Of all the people I'd known over the years, the Oracle was the one I'd known the longest. I even almost liked her. "I suppose you have something horrible to share?"

"I do like to bring you bad news." Amusement echoed in her voice.

"Please sit."

She collapsed in the chair, heaving a sigh. "I've found her."

"Her?"

"Her. Yes, her." She leaned forward, eyes intense. "The one who will thaw you."

I scowled at her. "That prophecy again?"

"*The* prophecy. At least, as far as you are concerned."

"I've told you—I'm fine as I am. And that prophecy is bloody nonsense."

"No, it is not. *You* are an animated block of ice who can barely see color or smell the night air or taste anything decent. And *she* will thaw you."

"The curse is what it is. There is no cure."

"That is not true. Your immortality can be cured."

"What says I want it cured?"

She looked around the quiet office. "This, for eternity?"

"I've tried everything else." And I had. Sumptuous mansions, parties, lovers, every dangerous sport in the history of humanity.

Anything to pass the interminable years of immortality.

What the movies and books didn't understand was that immortality was a curse. Years upon years of the same thing, all of it experienced in a haze and punctuated only by the death of anyone you might grow to care for. It cast the world in shades of gray.

Born vampires didn't have to suffer it—they died and went to an afterlife like any normal creature. But turned vampires did. We were inhuman monsters, cursed to walk the earth forever. It made me good at business and miserable at everything else.

"I've accepted my lot, Oracle. You should, too."

"I won't accept a lie. And what I have seen is the truth. Her blood will make you feel alive again."

"It's all bloody nonsense," I said.

Quick as a quip, the Oracle leaned across the table and gripped my arm tight, forcing a vision into my mind. It burst to life—Carrow and me in vivid color. Her hair was golden, her lips red. Her lavender scent was so strong it made me dizzy, and I could imagine the taste of her so well. The air turned warm. Suddenly, I felt alive. The air around me vibrated with it. Everything vibrated with it.

The Oracle yanked her hand away, and the world returned to gray. Stale and cold.

I blinked at her. "Impossible."

"*Not* impossible."

"Is there something you aren't telling me?"

She shrugged, her gaze enigmatic. "If this whole thing is impossible, then you don't need to know, do you?"

She was right. It *was* impossible, so it didn't matter. I didn't have time for fairy tales. All the same, it felt like there was something she wasn't telling me.

∼

Carrow

I slept well that night, dreaming once again that Cordelia came to visit me. After the raccoon's help at the morgue, I knew I wanted to find her again. Something to add to my to-do list when I finally cleared my name.

Near noon, Mac woke me with coffee and more Oreos.

"This is a thing with you, isn't it?" I asked.

She chomped into a biscuit. "You'd better believe it is. Try dipping it in your coffee for a little something extra."

"I'll consider it."

After we'd finished eating, she leaned close. "I want to show you something."

"Yeah?" I raised an eyebrow.

She stood. "Come on."

I followed her to the door. She led me to the stairs outside her flat and turned right, heading up to the next floor. The door was unlocked, and she pushed it open, revealing a small, empty flat. It was charming, though, with wooden floors and white walls and a heavily beamed ceiling.

I looked at her. "Why are we here?"

"I thought you might want to give it a look. In case you wanted to move in."

She was the second person in less than a day to encourage me to leave the human world, and something about this place pulled at me so hard I could feel it.

"I'm going to leave you to it," Mac said. "Do a bit of thinking."

"I probably can't afford the rent."

"With skills like yours, you can."

"I don't know how to turn those skills into rent money."

She nudged my shoulder with hers. "We'll figure that out."

Before I could respond, she'd disappeared down the stairs, back to her flat. I turned, inspecting the space more closely. It was a million miles better than my place back in London. And right now, I was glad I didn't know how much it cost.

Maybe I could have an amazing new life in this magical world. With friends and fun and excitement, instead of merely surviving with my mini boxed wine and raccoon bestie.

My mobile buzzed, and dread uncoiled within me. I had so few friends in the real world—none, to be precise—that it had to be Corrigan.

The text message that popped up on the screen made my heart pitch.

There has been another murder and an abduction. One body left, one person taken. One witness who may be able to exonerate you. Turn yourself in now.

My heart began to race.

Shit, shit, shit.

Who *may* be able to exonerate me? That meant the witness hadn't gotten a good look. They might or might not be able to clear my name. I wanted my name cleared. More importantly, I wanted to find Beatrix's killer. Even more importantly, someone had been abducted.

Someone could still be alive.

I had to find them.

Now.

I spun toward the door, determined to find the Devil and get a move on.

He stood in the doorway, looking cold and perfect as ever, but there were shadows under his eyes that made him look almost human.

Had he had a bad night?

I shook the thought away. It didn't matter. "Thank God you're here."

His brows rose. "I can't say I mind the enthusiasm."

"That's not it. The police have evidence that the killer has struck again. And someone has been abducted."

"Then you'll be glad to know that Remington's potion has found a location."

Relief surged through me. "Let's go. We need to be in time."

The Devil nodded and turned to leave. I followed him, giving the flat a last longing look as I headed down the stairs. I peeked into Mac's flat, but she wasn't there. I'd tell her everything when I got back.

When we reached the street, we nearly ran into Quinn. He was dressed for a jog, looking handsome and disheveled. His cheeks glowed with healthy color, and every bit of him looked a world away from the Devil's cold, hard strength.

"Are you all right, Carrow?" Quinn's eyes sharpened on the man next to me. Suddenly, I could see the panther in his soul.

Any other man might have quailed under the Devil's frigid glare. My companion stepped closer to me, raising one eyebrow. "We need to be on our way."

"I'm fine, Quinn." I touched his arm to reassure him and immediately felt the weight of the Devil's stare on my hand.

He didn't want me to touch Quinn. He didn't like it.

I glanced quickly at the Devil, certain that I spotted jealousy in his eyes.

No way. That wasn't possible.

I turned back to Quinn. "I'll see you later. We need to run."

"I'll be at the bar. Check in when you get back, so I know you're safe."

"She'll be fine." The Devil's voice was as icy as his demeanor.

"I'd like to see for myself."

What the hell was happening?

Were two enormous, handsome, powerful men fighting over me?

Because that was sure as hell what it felt like. And boy, was that unusual.

"Be careful." Quinn gave me one last look before he turned and entered his building.

"Come on." The Devil's voice was cold, but the chill I heard was not directed at me. It was almost as if he could shoot icicles at Quinn's retreating back.

Together, we strode in silence toward the city gate. I didn't mention the encounter or ask the Devil about his behavior. Underneath his cool exterior, I sensed that he'd surprised himself. Or maybe I was making that up.

Seeing the two of them together had been a revelation, though.

If I were wise, I'd be interested in Quinn. Handsome, strong, clever, nice.

Instead, I wanted the Devil of Darkvale—also handsome and strong and clever, but scary and powerful and cold and mysterious.

Idiot.

I sneaked a glance at him, noting the way the sunlight gleamed off his dark hair. Hang on... "You can go in the sunlight?"

"Did you expect me to burst into flame?"

"Maybe."

"No, that only happens in a church."

"Really?"

"Also no."

I grumbled. "Where are we headed?"

"London. Your London."

Damn. I didn't have a face-concealing potion, and

there wasn't time to find one. Not if we wanted to save this person, whoever they were. I'd just have to keep my head ducked.

Instead of going to the gate that Mac and I had been using, the Devil led me to the other side of town, back toward his club.

I frowned. "The gate isn't this way."

"I use a private gate."

I raised my brows. "You're the only one?"

He nodded.

I hadn't been in Guild City long, but even I knew that had to be a big deal.

The Devil led me toward the tower that contained his bar and, presumably, his home.

"Have you lived here long?" I asked as we approached the two guards at the door.

"A while."

"That's a non-answer."

He shot me a rare smile. "You're clever."

"I know I am, now answer the question."

"Too late." He gestured to the guards, who stood only several meters away. "We've arrived."

They opened the doors, and we strode in. The Devil nodded at the hostess, then led me down several halls. We bypassed the club portion entirely, sticking to the dimly lit passageways that were currently empty. I wondered where he lived in here—it certainly couldn't be his office, and the place was huge—but there were no clues.

We reached an unassuming black door a moment later, and he pressed his hand to it. I could feel the faintest swell of magic in the air—it seemed to take my breath away, like the downward plunge on a roller coaster—and the door disappeared.

"Come." He stepped through first, and I followed.

Magic seemed to suck me in, and a moment later, I stood in a dark alley.

"We're near the Haunted Hound," he said. "Only a few streets away."

"How do we find our guy?"

The Devil pulled a small compass from his pocket. I peered at it more closely, realizing that it wasn't marked with north and south like a normal compass. There were no headings at all, in fact. Instead, the little red dial just pointed forward and slightly to the left.

"Let's go." The Devil strode away, and I followed him.

As we exited the alley onto a busy street full of shops and restaurants, I pulled my hood up to conceal my hair. I kept my chin tucked as I walked and stayed close to the Devil. We left Covent Garden and walked farther, finally reaching a shadier neighborhood that wasn't nearly as nice. The crowd had thinned out, and the quality of the restaurants and bars had severely declined.

The neighborhoods had one thing in common,

though: my face, plastered on posters in several windows.

"We're not far now," he said.

"How can you tell?"

"It vibrates as we get closer." The Devil pointed to a shoddy-looking pub on the corner. "I think that's our target."

Just beyond the pub, a policeman stood with his back to us. We were only about ten meters apart, and if he came this way…

As if he could sense my discomfort, the Devil said, "You're worried he'll recognize you from the wanted posters."

"Yes."

The policeman shifted as if he were about to turn, and I grabbed the Devil's arm. "Come on. Into this alley."

We darted into the narrow passageway, which was distressingly empty. There were no rubbish bins or old boxes to hide behind, and it was tragically shallow. The Devil peeked around the edge of the building to check on the policeman, then ducked back in.

"He's coming." His serious gaze met mine. "I can take care of him."

"No." Whatever the Devil would do to him wouldn't be good, even if he didn't hurt him. I didn't want him using his mind control power on some unsuspecting policeman.

An idea flared to life.

Excitement and fear rushed through me as I grabbed the Devil by the jacket and pulled him closer to me. His firelight scent wrapped around me, and he towered a good head over me.

"Pretend to kiss me," I said.

"Pretend?"

My gaze flicked up to meet his, and the heat in his eyes made my muscles go weak. His broad shoulders blocked the light at the end of the alley, and his head was bent low. He rested his hands on the brick wall on either side of my head, caging me in.

"Yeah." My voice was rusty as I spoke. "Pretend."

He dipped his head to my neck, his lips hovering over my skin. The faint brush of his breath made me tremble.

"Put your arms around me," he murmured. "So the cop will think you want to be here."

A shiver raced through me. Oh, I *very* much wanted to be there. My solo nights with an adult juice box and Cordelia were nothing compared to this. To say I'd been in a drought was an understatement.

I wrapped my arms around his back, making sure they were over his jacket so that the cop could see them if he looked in. We needed to hide our faces, but we didn't want to get hauled in for public indecency.

"That's it," he murmured, his lips brushing against my skin.

I shivered again, heat racing through my veins. I wanted him to kiss me. To press his lips firmly against me, to feel his touch.

A shudder ran through him, and I gripped him more tightly.

17

The Devil

Holding Carrow in my arms was heaven, or as close as I'd ever get to paradise.

It was also hell.

The scent of her was a drug, making my head spin as I resisted sinking my fangs into her neck. It would be so sweet, so perfect.

A shudder ran over me.

Resist.

But I had to have something. She called to me like a siren.

Unable to help myself, I pressed my lips to the smooth, warm skin of her neck.

A soft rush of breath escaped her as she tilted her

head to the right, giving me more access. A low groan was torn from my throat, and I pressed against her, nearly forgetting the cop that we were hiding from. My lips parted.

Just one taste.

When my tongue touched her skin, it was bliss.

A moan of pleasure escaped her.

"All right, all right," the cop's voice sounded from behind us. Protectiveness surged through me, but when I heard his voice again, it drifted from down the street, and I realized that he'd kept walking as he talked. "Break it up, lovebirds. Not too much in the daylight."

In my arms, Carrow sagged. She dropped her head back against the brick wall and looked up to meet my gaze. "That was close."

"It was." My voice was oddly rough as I spoke.

I forced myself to pull back.

I'd kissed her skin. For fate's sake, I'd *licked* her.

I hadn't done that in centuries.

Shocked by my own actions, I turned and looked out of the alley. The cop was turning down another street. "He's gone."

"Good." Carrow's voice was nearly back to normal. "Let's go get our guy."

She strode out onto the street, and I joined her. I pulled the magical compass out of my pocket and held it in front of me. The arrow spun and stopped, pointing at the ramshackle pub at the end of the street. The little thing vibrated fiercely in my hands, indicating that we were nearly there.

"Is he really in a human pub?" she asked. "Just sitting and drinking? What about the abduction?"

"It does seem odd." I inspected the dreary surroundings. "Some places in the human world are actually secret supernatural hot spots, like the Haunted Hound, but I don't think this is one of them."

"This is just too strange." She leaned over and looked at the compass, which was still buzzing.

We stopped in front of the wooden door. It was impossible to see through the dirty glass, but I could feel our prey on the other side. It was a vampire instinct.

"He's inside." I raised my wrist to my mouth and spoke into the comms charm strapped there, calling for backup from my shifter bodyguards.

"What was that for?"

"Just in case. They'll wait outside unless I call them in."

"Right, then. Let's figure out why the hell our target is in a pub."

∾

Carrow

We were about to catch this bastard.

My name would be cleared soon. Lives would be saved. *Finally*, I'd be in time to save someone. If we caught this guy, the deaths would stop.

Heart pounding, I moved to push the door open, but the Devil was faster. He stepped into the pub first, blocking me from any threat. I followed, my eyes quickly adjusting to the dim light. Every inch of me was on the alert—to flee, to attack, I wasn't sure.

But the pub was...normal. Gloomy and dingy, there was almost no one inside. Still, my gaze went unerringly to the guy sitting at the bar alone. The bartender stood on the far side, giving the guy a wide berth.

The Devil nodded to the seated man. "It's him."

"Really? He seems so...normal." Not like a necromancer at all.

"He's human. No magic that I can feel. Not even well controlled magic."

"But he still committed the murder?" I could hear the faint buzz from the magical compass that the Devil held.

"Yes. He may be a hired gun."

I looked back at the man, anger bubbling inside me.

He was tall, with broad shoulders and a partially bald head. His plain white T-shirt was covered in dark stains that I initially took for blood.

No way.

I blinked, realizing it was probably engine grease.

Still, he had Beatrix's blood on his hands. Anger seethed inside me like a snake, twisting and writhing.

As if he could feel the intensity of our scrutiny, the man turned to look at us. Moving in synchrony, as though we'd been partners for years, the Devil and I approached the bar and seated ourselves on either side of him. I clenched my fists to keep from punching him.

The man turned to look at me, his heavy bulldog's face creased in a scowl. "What do you want?"

Heart pounding, I returned his stare.

Our suspect.

The murderer.

I could feel it, just like I'd suspected I might.

The Devil gripped the back of the man's neck. "Look at me."

The man flailed in his grasp. The Devil's knuckles whitened, and the bastard stilled.

The bartender took a hasty step back, moving away from the confrontation.

I didn't blame him. The Devil looked so ruthless that even I didn't want to be near him right now, and he was on my side.

"Tell me about the murders you committed," the Devil said.

"Where is the abducted person?" I cut in. I was desperate to know about Beatrix—but there was a living person's life on the line. They had to come first.

The Devil tightened his hold on the man. "Answer her."

"I have no idea what—"

"Answer truthfully." The Devil's voice lowered, and magic sparked in the air around him.

"It was a job, all right?" The words seemed torn from the man. "Just a job I was paid for."

As we'd thought—he wasn't the mastermind. Helpless rage twisted inside me at the idea that another person was out there, and that Beatrix's murder had been *just a job*.

"Murder isn't *just* a job," I said, voicing my thoughts aloud.

"It is for me."

"Where is the person you abducted?" I demanded.

"I don't know!"

"It's the truth." The Devil's voice was grim.

No. I couldn't accept that. "Where do you think they are? Any clues? Anything at all."

"I don't know. The client mentioned something about a church."

Just like the Devil had said. Flares of dark magic coming from different churches. "Which church?"

"I don't know. I don't care about churches, so I didn't recognize it."

"You've been there?" I asked.

"What if I have?"

"Where was it?"

"Somewhere in the city. Maybe near Fleet Street. Don't know exactly. The client's guys took me there to meet him, but I was blindfolded."

Damn it.

I drew in a bracing breath, then reached out and touched his shoulder. A wave of disgusting energy flowed into me, making my stomach pitch. Sometimes, when I touched something with a particularly vile past, I could feel it. And this guy had a *very* vile past. I prayed I wouldn't see Beatrix's death.

Flashes of the recent murders ran through my mind…a club coming down on the first man's head. A blade plunging into a chest. It made me ill. Cold chills raced over me, and my insides turned to snakes.

I swayed on my seat. The Devil gripped my shoulder, steadying me. I relaxed against his hand, absorbing his strength as I drew an unsteady breath.

The church…the church.

I had to see the church he'd been to.

But it was impossible to call up certain images or information. My gift showed me whatever *it* wanted, not whatever *I* wanted.

"The church, man." The Devil's words were harsh, and his magic flared in the air. "Think of the church."

He knew what I was trying to do. I gave him a grateful smile.

A moment later, an image of the church flashed in my mind. Moderately sized, situated right in the middle of London. A small cemetery surrounded it, packed in between the tall buildings. But the building itself was unusual, with curving walls. I'd never seen a church shaped like that. Not here, at least.

Contact with the murderer was making me so woozy that it was nearly impossible to stay upright on the chair. I withdrew my hand from the man's arm, sucking in some of the stale pub air.

"Is the abducted person still alive?" I demanded.

"Yes. He wanted her for a ceremony. Had to bring her alive for it."

Her.

He'd abducted a woman.

"When will the ceremony be?" I asked.

"On the full moon," the man said. "Midnight."

"Tonight," the Devil murmured.

"What does he want her for?" I demanded.

The man shrugged violently. "Why would I know?"

"Because you did the dirty work."

"Just a job, lady."

"Not just a job," the Devil said, repeating my words. "What organ did you take from your last victim?"

Oh, that was a good question.

The man's jaw clenched. Clearly, he didn't want to answer.

"Tell me." The Devil's words were cold enough to freeze lava.

"The liver," the murderer said.

"Why?" I asked.

"Because I was told to. Gave it to the creepy bloke, along with the woman."

"What was the woman's name?" I asked.

"Don't know. Some lady about forty years old. He's not particular."

"What about the other victims?" the Devil asked. "Did it matter who you killed?"

"No. He just wanted the liver and heart."

"Why?" I snapped.

"Don't know."

"What did he look like?" the Devil asked.

"Never saw his face. Bloke wore a cape the whole time. Hood covered everything."

"Do you remember anything distinct about him?"

"No."

I looked at the murderer, feeling tightness in my throat. "Last year, did you kill a blonde girl with a raven tattooed on her back?"

The Devil growled. "Tell the truth."

The man's brow furrowed as he looked at me. "Yeah, I killed her for the client. He wanted another heart. What of it?"

Bile surged in my throat. My fist flashed up, and I punched him square in the face.

He slumped backward, unconscious, and I shook out my fist. "I want to kill him."

The Devil nodded and dropped the murderer. He

collapsed off his bar stool. "You can do so later, if you want."

I drew in an unsteady breath, knowing that he meant it. I'd never do it, though. As much as I wanted to pay him back for what he had done to Beatrix, committing murder myself wasn't the answer. I'd figure this out after we saved the other woman.

I looked toward the window. It was nearing dusk, and tonight was the full moon. I looked at the Devil. "We don't have long."

The Devil nodded and climbed off his stool, then patted down the unconscious man.

"What are you looking for?" I asked.

"The dagger."

"Oh, of course. Sorry I knocked him out before you could ask him. I was just so…"

"Angry." The Devil stood, an expression of understanding on his face. "I get it. Don't worry, the dagger isn't important."

"Thanks." I shook my arms, trying to drive off some of the tension I felt.

The Devil spoke into the little magical gadget strapped to his wrist. "Come into the pub. There's someone you need to pick up."

At my feet, the murderer groaned and staggered to his feet The Devil grabbed him by the arm. The bastard jerked away, but the Devil was too fast.

He pulled him close, his teeth bared. "Run and I will

tear your throat out," he said in a low, calm voice that sent shivers down my spine.

The man wilted.

I didn't blame him.

"And this is for Carrow's friend, Beatrix." The Devil punched him hard in the face, knocking him cold, and let the body fall.

"Thanks." I appreciated that punch more than a million roses.

The Devil nodded, glaring contemptuously at the hitman at his feet.

Two enormous men walked into the pub, each dressed in dark trousers and commando sweaters. Tactical wear, if I had to call it anything. They strode toward the Devil.

"Is this the guy, boss?" one of the men asked. He had wavy auburn hair and broad, handsome features and reminded me of a lion. His shifter form, if I had to bet.. I thought I recognized him from the Devil's office the first day I'd met him.

"Yes. Take him back and hold him for further questioning."

The Devil's shifter bodyguards dragged the man out of the pub. The Devil turned toward the bartender, who raised his hands and shrank against the shelves of liquor bottles. "I won't say anything, I swear," the poor man babbled.

"No, you won't speak of this to anyone. You will

forget it immediately." I could feel the Devil's magic in the air, and the man's eyes went blank as he nodded.

"Good man." The Devil turned to me. "Now, what do you say we go save this woman and finish getting your vengeance?"

18

CARROW

There were still six hours until midnight, and I insisted on going back to the Haunted Hound immediately. I couldn't linger on the streets of London, and we were closer to that gate than to the Devil's.

As we walked, images of the murderer flashed in my mind.

"You all right?" the Devil asked.

"Just glad we got him." I drew in a shuddery breath. "I want to kill him. And the damn necromancer who hired him."

"We'll get him, too. I promise."

Oh, we would. I didn't relish the thought of blood on

my hands, but if I had to kill the necromancer, I'd do it with delight.

We reached the alley only a few minutes later, and returning to the magical world felt as natural as breathing. I pressed my hands to the dingy, unwelcoming door of the Haunted Hound, and the magic admitted me, swinging the door open.

I looked back at the Devil, wondering if he would look uncomfortable, since he was clearly on Quinn's turf.

No, he didn't.

Of course he didn't. Nothing made him uncomfortable.

He strode into the crowded little pub like he owned the place. Quinn stood behind the bar, along with Mac, who wiped down the gleaming wood with a cloth. My friends avoided the Devil's gaze, looking at me instead from across the room.

"Are you okay?" Quinn asked.

"Did you get your target?" Mac set down the rag and leaned on the bar.

"Yes to both," I said. "Mostly."

I approached the bar, the Devil at my side.

"Fancy seeing you here," Quinn said to him.

"You're right. I should get out more." The Devil's words were dry.

"Update us, already," Mac demanded.

I told them about the hired gun and the necromancer, then asked, "Do you have a piece of paper? We need to find a church, and I don't recognize it from the vision I had. Maybe you will."

Quinn nodded and disappeared to the back. He returned a moment later with a notepad and pencil and pushed them toward me.

I was a terrible artist, but I did my best to sketch the church from memory. I was most interested in capturing the curved walls and low, almost flat dome, which seemed like the most identifiable parts of the church.

My three companions leaned over the bar as I worked, watching the place come to life. I was painfully aware of the Devil at my side. There was a good half-meter between us, but the air between us tingled with something magical. My whole body was alive with awareness of him.

Finally, I finished and sat back, staring at the drawing. I blinked at it. Now that I'd drawn it all out... "I think I recognize it. Is that Temple Church near the Inns of Court?"

"I think it is," Quinn said.

"But it's a church for humans." I said. It had been built in the twelfth century by the Knights Templar. "Would a necromancer really go there?"

"Some places are multi-use, yes," the Devil said. "He would cast a spell to keep humans away, most likely. But there are many places in the human realm that are imbued with great magic. This is likely one of them."

I stared at the picture. "And at midnight, he's probably going to ritualistically murder our abducted person to create some kind of deadly magic."

"I'll see if Miranda can find out what kind of necromancy can be accomplished with a heart, a liver, and a living victim."

Just the idea made me shudder, but I nodded.

"So what are we going to do?" Mac said. "Ambush the church?"

I looked at her gratefully. "You don't have to come."

"Of course I do. You need help, and you're my friend."

Warmth surged through me. "Thanks."

"I'll close down the pub," Quinn said.

"Thank you." I wasn't going to refuse an any offer of help. A woman's life was at stake, and I still needed vengeance for Beatrix.

~

At eleven p.m., we took up our places near Temple Church. The church sat in the middle of a small graveyard surrounded by tall buildings, the entire thing behind a gate that we'd had to climb over. The Devil and I stood in the shadows alongside Mac, Eve, and Quinn. Eve's raven sat in a nearby tree. I touched the bag of potion bombs that Eve had given me, grateful for the magical backup.

The Devil had brought his own security, half a dozen shifters crouched in the shadows in human form. I'd briefly spotted Quinn chatting with them, and he'd fit in like a pea in a pod. There was a certain energy about him when he was with the pack that made his shifter qualities evident.

"I think I see someone coming." The Devil murmured the words against my ear, and I shivered.

"Where?"

"To your right."

I looked in the direction he indicated, spotting a couple walking down the street. They would have had to have come over the gate, too, so they definitely weren't supposed to be there. I tucked myself deeper into the shadows to watch them approach. Two men, both of average height and looks.

"I think I recognize them," Mac murmured. "A seer and a sorcerer from Guild City. They pass through the pub sometimes but rarely stop to drink."

They reached the edge of the small graveyard and hesitated briefly. I squinted as I watched them, the full moon illuminating their movements. They gestured—a kind of circular movement with a flick at the end. The faintest flash of light appeared, and they stepped forward.

For a brief minute, the air around them turned a faint blue. Then they were on the other side of the barrier, and it disappeared.

"A magical shield," Eve whispered. "Only supernaturals can enter the graveyard as long as it is up."

"And only if they make that gesture," Quinn said.

The figures were blurry now, the barrier seeming to make them almost invisible to the eye. Someone walking by probably wouldn't notice them.

I strained my eyes, trying to glean any more clues about what was going on inside. We were only an hour from midnight, the most dangerous time for our victim. We didn't want to rush in and scare off the necromancer and lose her, so we were trying to play it slow and careful.

It was making me antsy as hell, though.

"They're putting something on," Quinn murmured.

As I watched, the blurry figures swirled cloaks around their shoulders and pulled up the hoods.

"Okay, that's some creepy ritual stuff," Mac said.

"Incoming," the Devil whispered.

I looked up, spotting two women headed toward us—incredibly gorgeous women like Eve, who had stashed her wings when we'd come to the human world, magically folding them into her body.

"Are they Fae?" I asked.

"They are." Eve's voice had a dark timbre. "Vivia and Elona. I never liked them."

They entered the protected graveyard in the same way the seer and the sorcerer had, using identical gestures. They were nearly invisible on the other side, but I caught sight of them sweep on their cloaks.

"It looks like someone from every guild is here," the Devil said. "Almost."

"Is it a council thing?" I asked.

"No. None of them are high ranking," Quinn said. "I wonder how many more are coming."

"It's close to midnight." I frowned. "Maybe not many more will show."

"It's a small church," the Devil said. "I'm not sure all of us will be able to sneak in unnoticed."

"You and I will go." I didn't mind risking him as much as my new friends...right? The idea made me uncomfortable, but there was no disputing the value of his abilities. And somehow, I knew he wouldn't let me go in there without him. I looked at Quinn, Eve, and Mac, who were scowling at me. "You guys can be backup if a fight starts."

"How will we know if a fight starts?" Mac said.

"I'll call you." If I had time.

"Bad idea." Mac shook her head and yanked off the necklace she wore, handing it to me. "Take my comms charm. When it gets dicey in there, tap it and call us. It's connected to Quinn's and Eve's charms, so we'll hear you."

"I can call my security force as backup as well," the Devil said.

"Okay. We're as prepared as we'll ever be, then." I

studied the street around us. "Let's slip into the graveyard and try to ambush the next people to arrive. We can use their cloaks to sneak in."

The Devil nodded. I gave my friends a goodbye look, then hurried after him toward the graveyard. When we reached the magical barrier, I could feel it prickle against my skin.

"Do you remember the symbol?" the Devil asked.

"I do." Raising my hand, I mimicked the circular gesture that I'd seen people make. The magic in the air changed slightly, and I held my breath as I stepped through the barrier. At first, it resisted. I had to force my foot through air that felt like jelly, but finally, I was inside the protected space.

The Devil entered with seeming ease and pointed to a massive headstone. "Let's hide there. We'll be covered and have a view of the church."

Together, we knelt behind the gravestone. The Devil had changed into the same simple black tactical wear that his security force wore, and somehow, he was even more handsome in casual clothing. My shoulder pressed against his thin jumper, and it was impossible not to feel the heat of his skin. Every inch of me was impossibly aware of him.

He was so still that I couldn't help but wonder if he was just as focused on me. I stole a look at him, and tension fizzed in the air between us. It took everything I had to direct my attention toward the path.

A third pair of people approached, though it was hard to make out their forms through the magical barrier. Fortunately, the barrier worked in both directions, blurring the figures within and without.

A moment later, they'd crossed through the barrier, and I got a good look at them. They were a man and a woman, each with average features but of similar height to the Devil and me, respectively.

They stopped and withdrew two red cloaks from their bags. I was bracing myself to lunge from our hiding space when the Devil moved. He was beside them in a blur and smashed their heads together.

They dropped to the ground, unconscious, and he dragged them by their feet to our hiding space.

I gaped at him. "Holy crap, you're fast."

His gaze flicked up to me, and something darkened in his eyes. "Being a monster has its benefits."

Like super speed and super strength. But it was his use of the word *monster* that caught my ear. There was an edge to it that I didn't understand. Not that I had time to be mulling over such things.

The Devil quickly bound the two figures with their belts and shoelaces, then tore strips from their shirts and gagged them. Last, he raised his wrist to his mouth and spoke into his comms charm. "Rafe? Cleanup in the graveyard, two bodies. We'll put them in the cells before turning them over to the guild."

"Cells?" I grabbed one of the cloaks and tugged it on.

"Another perk of being a monster."

He owned cells.

I pushed the thought aside. The tall, dark figure of Rafe appeared a moment later, along with his partner, both moving with leonine grace. As the Devil put on his red cloak, they disappeared with the two bodies.

His face was shadowed as he met my gaze. "Ready to wing it?"

"Ready." My heart raced.

Together, we approached the main door of the church. It was nearly midnight now, and anxiety flooded my veins. The massive wooden doors gave way with smooth ease beneath our touch, and we stepped inside the church. It echoed with a silence that seemed to scream through the space.

I took it all in as quickly as I could, not wanting to hesitate too long. Hesitation might reveal that I had no idea what I was doing.

That I wasn't one of them.

Unfortunately, the main doors led directly into the circular, domed space—right where everyone else was standing. Nearly three dozen cloaked figures stood around the perimeter of the room, staring silently at the empty altar in the middle.

There were so many.

Fear pierced me, and I nearly clutched the Devil's hand for support. I didn't, of course. This was not the place for hand-holding, no matter how much I wanted to cling to him for safety. No matter what, I couldn't break character and give us away.

I couldn't find the victim amongst the crowd, and no one stood out as the leader. Everyone was identical in their red cloaks, hidden by their cowardice and evil.

I was deeply grateful Beatrix hadn't seen any of this. We'd found her body intact, and she hadn't suffered long.

I kept my head tilted down as I walked alongside the Devil. If everyone was meant to stand equidistant, that meant that there were two spaces empty across the room. We were possibly the last to arrive.

Together, we strode toward the empty spaces in the lineup. My heartbeat thundered in my ears as we walked, and I prayed that no one was watching too closely. The cloaks covered our faces, but if someone looked from the right angle, they might penetrate our disguises.

Once we were in place, I surreptitiously looked around. It was nearly impossible to make out anyone's features, and no one looked like the leader. Was the necromancer with the victim now?

Would he bring her out?

The ground began to vibrate, and I stiffened.

Magical signatures filled the air, sparking through the space. There were all sorts of scents and sounds, tastes and feelings. Most of them were bad—the smell of burning rubber, the taste of rotten fruit, the smell of sewage. It felt prickly and evil, like a million ants crawling along my skin.

But it was the smell of death that made my skin grow cold.

The necromancer was coming.

19

CARROW

Temple Church vibrated with power. All around, people raised their hands. Immediately, I mimicked the gesture. The magic flared even stronger, and I realized that these people were feeding their power into the air.

I shared the briefest glance with the Devil, and he shook his head faintly.

Did he mean that I shouldn't try to mimic what they were doing? I wasn't even sure if I *could* push my magic into the air. And if I did, would they be able to sense that I wasn't the person I was supposed to be?

A low chant began, each person in the room humming notes that made the hair raise on my arms. Magic surged toward the altar, swirling around the great stone platform. Their voices rolled like thunder, vibrating in my chest.

The air shimmered, and a woman appeared, lying still on the dais. She appeared unconscious—*please don't be dead*—and her hands and legs were bound. Next to her, a man's form fizzled into existence.

Unlike the others' cloaks, his was black. The magic rolling off him made the other participants seem almost nice in comparison.

The necromancer.

Rage seethed through me at the sight of him. He was the real reason Beatrix had been murdered. The reason this other poor woman was on the slab. He raised his hands and began to chant in a rumbling voice. His magic rolled over me, and my stomach pitched. I felt like I was suddenly swimming in acid.

How the hell were we going to fight all these people? We were drastically outnumbered.

But that woman...

I couldn't look away from her.

She didn't stand a chance unless we intervened, and it was only going to get more difficult as time went on.

I drew an unsteady breath, trying to brace myself, and murmured to the Devil, "We need to attack. Now."

Quick as a snake, he raised his wrist to his lips and whispered a command. I caught the word *now*. The shifters were coming. I pressed my hand to my comms charm and repeated the word, alerting my friends.

The Devil attacked without warning. He slammed his fist into the stone slabs that made up the floor, sending a reverberation of power through the tiles. Somehow, it avoided me, but every other person in the room lost their balance and collapsed to the ground.

Only the necromancer remained standing, and his chants grew louder.

His followers scrambled to right themselves, but the Devil was in motion. He charged the nearest one, landing a devastating punch that slammed the cloaked figure against the wall. His speed was incredible, and he was already moving to the next.

I plunged my hand into the bag at my side, drawing out a potion bomb. I had no idea which one it was, but they were all designed for this kind of fight. I hurled the glass orb at the necromancer. It flew through the air, smashed into an unseen barrier, and disintegrated.

Shit!

The necromancer raised his hands over the woman's body and kept chanting. Two bloody organs appeared, floating over her chest.

The heart and liver from the other victims.

Fear and revulsion surged through me.

As I fumbled in my bag for another potion bomb, the two organs began to glow. Magic swirled around them, dark and glittery, transforming them into something else, but what?

The Devil moved with deadly efficiency around the

room. The other cloaked figures staggered up, calling on their magic and turning it against him. Fireballs whizzed toward me. The Devil intercepted them, taking the hits without so much as faltering. He seemed to absorb the attacking magic, growing stronger with every blow.

The Devil's security team and my friends burst into the church, spreading out to attack. Magic flashed as the shifters transformed into powerful beasts—a bear, a lion, a tiger, and three wolves. In the flash of an eye, Quinn transformed into a massive golden panther. He roared and lunged for a cloaked figure, while Mac drew her sword and charged another. The eight of them moved quickly, going for the supernaturals who fought back with magic that flashed and boomed through the church.

Eve's glittering wings appeared behind her, and she launched herself into the air, flying high as she raised her hands and shot lightning from her palms. She aimed for the necromancer, but her attack was deflected by the invisible shield that protected him.

In front of him, the glowing organs had shrunk in size, combining to form a shining red jewel. Magic radiated from it, dark and terrifying. Slowly, the gem lowered toward the woman.

Triumph radiated from the necromancer. The gem was a weapon. If it reached her, this was all over.

Damn it. We had to get past that shield.

The Devil seemed to agree. As the battle raged around us, he charged the necromancer. He moved like a steam train, so fast and powerful that he plowed through the barrier. Magic exploded from him, sending me flying, and I crashed against the wall in a flare of pain.

By the time I got back to my feet, he had the necromancer by the neck. Both were on their knees, and much of the Devil's skin was blackened by an oily substance.

I sprinted for them. A red-cloaked figure nearly collided with me, but Quinn shoved his massive panther body between me and danger.

I reached the Devil in time to hear him demand, "Make it stop."

To the left of him and the necromancer, the glowing gem lowered closer to the woman. By then, it was only half a meter above her chest.

"Make it stop," the Devil demanded. "Cease this magic."

"It can't be stopped," the necromancer hissed, blinking his eyes frantically to avoid the Devil's mind control power.

His hood had partially fallen away, revealing a pale-skinned man with sandy hair and burning black eyes. The Devil's face was twisted with pain and effort, and the black substance that covered his arms and chest seemed to be steaming, as if it were eating away at his skin.

Necromancer magic, and it was hurting him.

Killing him?

Something twisted in my chest—a weakness. Our connection was flickering, as if his life force was fading. Panic flared, worry screaming through me.

The necromancer's words were thick with triumph. "It is Orion's Heart, and once it is inside her, it will be complete."

The Devil's hand tightened on his neck, the knuckles turning white. "Stop the spell."

The necromancer's eyes began to fog.

Yes. The Devil's mind control was working. He would force him to stop this.

But the necromancer shook his head like a dog, as though shaking off the Devil's control. "Never," he said through gritted teeth. "My work here is done."

My skin chilled at his satisfaction.

He raised a hand, his dark cloak flapping around his arm, and slammed something into his mouth.

Immediately, his skin began to turn to ash. It looked like something out of a movie as his body crumbled and flaked away.

The Devil lurched back, his movements slow and sluggish. Weaker.

Holding the necromancer had grievously wounded him.

As for the necromancer, he'd turned into a pathetic pile of ash.

Dead. *No.*

Our answers were gone with him.

I spun toward the woman on the altar, the blood roaring in my ears. The necromancer's terrible gem was closing in, drawn to her still form. It was only centimeters away now. Asleep, she looked so peaceful and pretty, just a girl who had no idea that her entire life was at stake.

Terror for her opened a hole in my chest. I couldn't bear to watch her die, a victim to dark magic and evil. And what would happen if the necromancer's spell was complete?

We couldn't afford to find out.

I reached for the stone, but it was surrounded by flames. I screamed and jerked my hand backward. Too hot to touch.

I tried to push her off the altar, away from the stone, but she was protected by the same charm. The dark magic burned my hands fiercely, and I yanked them back. Damn it. *Damn it.* There had to be a way to stop this.

The Devil was incapacitated. Out of the corner of my eye, I could see him struggling to stand. All around, the fight raged. My friends were fighting to get to me, but there was no time.

I lunged for the pile of ashes that had once been the

necromancer, grabbing his charred cloak. Images flashed in my mind, sickening and terrible, turning my stomach. My gift was scrambling inside me, trying to find valuable information from the remnants of the man who had created this disaster.

Only the one who holds the stone can control it.

The message flashed in my mind, clear as day. I had to hold the stone.

The memory of the burning made my stomach lurch, but I ignored it. I lunged upright, moving for the altar.

"No." The Devil's voice was weak. He'd made it to his feet, but he was being poisoned by the black oil that covered him. "Let me."

I ignored him, stretching my hand out for the gem, determined to tear it away before it reached the girl.

Pain like I'd never known shot through my hand and up my arm. Tears stung my eyes, and sweat broke out on my skin. I pushed my hand harder, forcing it through the thick, agonizing air. It was like shoving my hand through a container full of glass.

A warm, solid weight pressed against my shin. I glanced down, spotting Cordelia. The little raccoon had appeared, gluing herself against my side. Warmth and strength flowed from her into me, giving me more power.

I pushed harder, and a scream tore from my throat as my hand closed around the gem.

Falling away, I landed on my back with the orb in my hand, then panted as I blinked up at the ceiling. The pain had stopped. My head spun as I sat up. On the altar, the girl lay still. I opened my palm. The red stone I held glowed with a faint light.

"What did you do?" The Devil's voice was a croak.

He stood before me, his face pale.

Then he collapsed to his knees.

I scrambled toward him, clutching the stone in my hand. "Are you okay? What's wrong with you?"

"I'm—" The words couldn't escape him.

Eve landed next to us, her glittery wings folding back into her body. "He's been poisoned by the necromancer." She dug a hand into one of her many pockets and pulled out a vial. She opened it, dumped the contents into her hand, and blew the powder on the Devil.

It coated him, and the oil began to disappear.

"Will that fix him?" I demanded.

In front of me, the Devil swayed, hardly able to stay upright.

"I think it's too late." Eve frowned, confusion flickering in her eyes. "The oil has sucked the life from him."

"But it's gone now. The oil is gone." Her powder had absorbed it all, leaving him looking clean and new. And pale. So damned pale. Even his eyes looked almost colorless.

"So is most of his life force."

"But—" I searched his face. Had he known this would happen when he'd blasted through the necromancer's protective shield and grabbed him?

Yes.

Somehow, I knew the answer was yes.

And I also knew how to fix him. My gaze flicked to his mouth, to his fangs that were now retracted.

Could I do this?

Yes.

The answer was yes.

I moved toward him, still gripping the gem that I didn't understand. Quickly, I wrapped my arms around him and bared my neck. His head dipped toward me as if he couldn't help it, a low groan tearing from his throat. But I didn't feel his teeth.

"Bite me," I demanded.

"Are you sure?" His voice was rough.

"You'll die without it, right?"

"I—will."

"Then bite me."

His lips pressed to my skin, and a shiver of fear and desire rushed through me. Was I really doing this?

His lips parted, and the air around us seemed to fog, filling with dark smoke. It formed a barrier between us and the world. I heard my friends cry out in concern, but I could no longer see them. Soon, I could no longer hear them.

We were in a cocoon, far away from them. The

Devil's magic protected us from the world so that no one could see us.

His warm breath brushed across my skin, and I shuddered. My heart raced, anticipation overwhelming. When his fangs pierced me, pleasure exploded. I moaned, moving closer to him until my chest was pressed to his.

20

The Devil

Carrow's arms wrapped around me, pulling me close as I drew on her neck. The feel of her beneath my hands, beneath my fangs, was enough to send my heart into overdrive.

She tasted so damned sweet. Everything I'd tasted since I'd been turned had been so damned dull.

But her...

Her scent swirled around me, lavender and something so intrinsically *her* that I couldn't get enough of it. The heady aroma was so much more powerful now.

I wrapped my hand around her waist and clutched her close, wanting to feel every part of her. It was unlike anything I'd ever experienced—even before I'd been turned.

The protective shield of my magic hid us from prying eyes, and I wanted more than this. I wanted to pull her clothes off, to taste her. I wanted to bury the years of loneliness in her. I was a seething mass of *want*.

Anything. I'd give anything to have her.

Beneath my lips, she tilted her head and moaned. The pleasure in the sound shot through me, and I clutched her closer. The connection between us surged, and it was impossible not to think of what the Oracle had said.

She would thaw me.

Was it possible?

Was the myth true?

With the taste of her blood on my tongue, it was impossible not to think so. Impossible not to believe it.

But the Oracle had been keeping secrets the day she'd come to see me—I could feel it.

"Grey."

The sound of my name on her lips made me shudder. I drew deeper on her neck, feeling my strength return.

Stop.

I had to stop.

With every bit of strength I gained, she lost some. She'd recoup it eventually, but if I drained her, she'd die.

With her taste sweet on my lips, I withdrew my mouth.

"Don't stop," she murmured, sounding half out of her mind.

"I must." I licked my lips, cleaning them of any trace of her, and cupped her face. "We have to stop."

Her eyes fluttered opened, and she looked at me.

Holy fates, her eyes were beautiful. Brilliant green. And her hair. An impossible gold.

Color.

I could see in color. Not just the faint shades of color that I'd been able to see before, but full blown *everything*. And the scents...

There were so many of them. I could taste the freshness of the air. And my skin felt more sensitive.

The Oracle had been correct.

She was the one who could make me whole again.

A thrill ran through me, followed by confusion and even fear. How the hell was this real?

"Are you better?" The strength was returning to her voice.

"I am. Thank you." I shoved aside thoughts of fate, forcing myself to my feet. I pulled her up alongside me, banishing the cloud of dark mist that hid us from her friends and my security force.

As the mist cleared, it revealed her three companions standing around us, anger and worry on their faces.

Behind them, my security force was working on binding the bodies of the necromancer's faithful. The Council of Guilds would owe me for this one.

They'd owe Carrow, too, though she didn't know it yet.

She gave me one last look, her gaze searching, then turned and hurried to the body of the woman on the slab. I could feel the life force inside the victim, and with any luck, she would have no memory of this.

Quinn strode up to me, back in his human form. His brow was creased with worry, and his eyes flickered with anger.

"Is there a problem?" I raised an eyebrow.

"I don't like what you did with her there."

"Too bad, because it is done." I so badly wanted to say that Carrow had enjoyed it, but I wouldn't reveal that information. It felt too personal. Too *hers*.

"Be careful."

The shifter's voice echoed with power, and I grinned. "You want her."

"And you don't?"

"Of course I do." I wasn't afraid to admit it.

His lips twisted. "I mean it. I'll be watching you. If you hurt her..."

"I understand." If it came down to a fight between us, I would win. But it wouldn't be easy. And it would cost me.

More likely than not, it *would* come down to a fight between us. Because I would hurt her. If I pursued her, I would hurt her. It was the only thing I was capable of. My past made that abundantly clear.

Disgusted with myself, I turned from the shifter and looked at Carrow. She was taking the woman's pulse and speaking with Mac and Eve. It was difficult to turn away from the sight of her. With my ability to see color returned, all I wanted to do was stare at her.

But I forced myself away. I was good at forcing myself away from the things I wanted. There was work to be done, after all, and I needed to begin. The dagger I'd been tracking was nowhere to be seen, but that wasn't my priority anymore.

I looked toward Carrow.

Getting the police off her back wouldn't be hard now that we had the real murderer. With a bit of mind control, the hired gun could be convinced to confess to his crimes. I just had to make sure it was all airtight.

I strode toward the head of my security force, determined to get it done quickly and protect her. Then I would leave her alone. No matter how damned hard it was, I would do that for her. I had to.

And yet, I knew there was no way I could say goodbye to her. Not a chance in hell.

Carrow

Three days later, it was finished. The necromancer was dead, and Beatrix's murderer would go to jail for his crimes. He had confessed, and the police had taken him into custody. I hadn't seen the Devil since he'd bitten me, but I'd heard through the grapevine that my name had been cleared with the police department. Corrigan had confirmed that Banks had led the charge against me with the wanted posters, and that he'd been reprimanded for bias.

I was no longer a wanted woman.

More importantly, the woman that we'd rescued was safe and sound, her memory wiped of everything bad.

Unfortunately, after the cops had searched my flat, someone had broken in and stolen everything. I'd taken it as a sign.

"I can't believe you're doing this." Mac grinned at me. "I'm so happy."

"Thanks for helping me figure it out." I looked at the green door that was now *our* green door. I held the key to the top-floor flat, right above Mac.

I'd cleared my name in the human world, but I didn't want to return. It was dim and miserable there, an awful half life where I tried to use my magic to help but ended up on the sidelines.

No. I wanted a new life—one full of color and excitement and friends. And the best way to have that was to move to Guild City. To the flat above Mac's, in fact. I was going to hang up my shingle as a mystery-solver of some kind. I still didn't know all the details, but I knew I was going to sell my services to those who needed them.

"You're going to do great," Mac said. "Your magic is so strong, everyone will want to hire you."

I had a reputation now, apparently. The fact that I'd held the necromancer's gem with my bare hand had gotten around town. We still didn't know exactly what the gem did, but it was powerful. So insanely powerful that it was supposed to be impossible to hold.

Yet I had.

I could still barely control my gift, but I could hold that gem.

I didn't understand it, but maybe one day, I would.

I'd considered handing the gem over to the Council of Guilds. I didn't want to possess something created from such darkness, no matter how powerful it was. But I didn't trust them, so I wore it on a chain around my neck. For now, at least.

"Go on." Mac gestured to the door. "Go check out your new place."

I smiled at her and turned the key in the lock. I took the stairs two at a time, leaving Mac at her place as I continued up to my own. As I pressed my hand to my door, the strongest sense of possibility yawned through me.

A grin stretched my face as I pushed open the door to my new flat.

It was as cheerful and bright as I remembered it, but two things caught my eye. A small stack of books in the middle of the floor ... and Cordelia.

The fat little raccoon looked at me, and a voice echoed in my mind. *Not a bad place we have here.*

I gaped at her. "You can talk?"

I'm your familiar. Of course I can talk.

"But...but..."

I like to dig through rubbish bins, but that doesn't mean you should make assumptions about my ability to hold a conversation.

"Um. True."

Mac appeared at my side, having followed me up the stairs.

She pointed to a pile of books on the floor. "What are those?"

I frowned in recognition. They were the ones that Beatrix had given me. The ones I'd had to leave behind at my old flat and hadn't been able to find after my name had been cleared. "Did you bring me those?"

No. That Devil bloke had them delivered.

Grey had them delivered?

My heartbeat fluttered. "She says the Devil delivered them."

"Oooh, I don't know about that," Mac said.

I looked at her. "What do you mean?"

"You heard what the Oracle said. He's dangerous to you. *Cursed Mates.*"

"You believe her?"

"Of course I do. Did you see her? She looks totally legit. And Fated Mates are a thing, so Cursed Mates could be one too."

"I *know* I'm not up for that kind of thing."

"Then you know what they say. Don't make a deal with the devil."

I nodded. I would avoid him. It was the only smart thing to do.

But more than ever, I had that feeling that we were two stars spinning through space, about to collide with each other. I would see him again. I was sure of it.

I thought of his bite, and how I wanted more. It was crazy, but I wanted more.

This was all happening too fast. Magic. A familiar. Gifts from a vampire. A new life.

I liked it.

I'd had a bite of this new life, and despite the danger and craziness of it, I wanted more.

I grinned at Cordelia and Mac. "How about a girls' night?"

A girls' night! I will consult the rubbish bins for a treat.

"Could do," I replied, leaning out the window to look

at the restaurant below. "But why don't we spring for a kebab? My treat, to celebrate our new life."

~~~

I hope you liked *Once Bitten!* Book two will be here next month. Sign up for my newsletter at www.Linsey-Hall.com to get info about when it comes out, as well as a novella about other characters in this world.

THANK YOU FOR READING!

I hope you enjoyed reading this book as much as I enjoyed writing it. Reviews are *so* helpful to authors. I really appreciate all reviews, both positive and negative. If you want to leave one, you can do so at Amazon or GoodReads.

ACKNOWLEDGMENTS

Thank you, Ben, for everything. There would be no books without you.

Thank you to Jena O'Connor, Lexi George, and Ash Fitzsimmons for your excellent editing. The book is immensely better because of you! And thank you to Maximillian, Susie, and Richard for your keen eye for errors.

Thank you to Orina Kafe for the beautiful cover art.

AUTHOR'S NOTE

Hey there! I hope you enjoyed *Once Bitten*. Most of the historical elements from this book were inspired by research trips to Romania and London. I often draw from history, and in cases where I modify it to suit the story, I like to share that.

The most important one to mention is the hero, the Devil of Darkvale, because he shares a name with someone but was not based specifically on that person. Vlad III Dracula (Vlad the Impaler) is Romania's greatest folk hero. He was the ruler of Wallachia, a region in Transylvania, three times during his life in the mid fifteenth century. During his life, he had no connections with vampirism, but his reputation for aggressive acts of violence on behalf of his region inspired the name of Bram Stoker's *Count Dracula* (published 1897).

He is a historical figure who is greatly admired for protecting his people, though the way he accomplished this often seems gruesome.

I have obviously gone in the same direction as Bram Stoker — using the name as inspiration for my vampire hero but not the actual person. As with Bram Stoker, my hero is not inspired by the real Vlad III Dracula, just by the myths.

For this story, nearly every aspect of my Vlad the Impaler is the product of my imagination, but Guild City is based upon his birthplace of Sighișoara in Transylvania. It is a beautiful medieval city surrounded by a roughly circular wall that is listed as a UNESCO World Heritage Site. As with Guild City, there are towers built into the wall that were once owned and maintained by various guilds (such as the tailors, bookmakers, butchers, tinsmiths, and rope makers). The guild towers were responsible for the defense of the city when it came under attack, and each one is different and fascinating. As soon as I as I saw them, I was imaging Guild City.

On the English side of things, Temple Church is based upon a real church in London that I visited with the author C.N. Crawford (so if you like my books, you may want to check out hers). It has a rich history, starting with its construction by the Knight's Templar in the twelfth century.

That's it for the history and myth in this book,

though I will go into more detail about the very cool guild towers in future books. Thank you for reading, and I hope you stick around with Carrow and the Devil to find out more.

ABOUT LINSEY

Before becoming a writer, Linsey Hall was a nautical archaeologist who studied shipwrecks from Hawaii and the Yukon to the UK and the Mediterranean. She credits fantasy and historical romances with her love of history and her career as an archaeologist. After a decade of tromping around the globe in search of old bits of stuff that people left lying about, she settled down and started penning her own romance novels. Her Dragon's Gift series draws upon her love of history and the paranormal elements that she can't help but include.

COPYRIGHT

This is a work of fiction. All reference to events, persons, and locale are used fictitiously, except where documented in historical record. Names, characters, and places are products of the author's imagination, and any resemblance to actual events, locales, or persons, living or dead, is coincidental.

Copyright 2020 by Linsey Hall

Published by Bonnie Doon Press LLC

All rights reserved, including the right of reproduction in whole or in part in any form, except in instances of quotation used in critical articles or book review. Where such permission is sufficient, the author grants the right to strip any DRM which may be applied to this work.

Linsey@LinseyHall.com

www.LinseyHall.com

https://www.facebook.com/LinseyHallAuthor